# Dream of Darkness

## The Rise of the Light, Volume 1

### H. M. Gooden

Published by H. M. Gooden, 2017.

DREAM OF DARKNESS

**First edition. October 15, 2017.**

Written by H. M. Gooden.

To everyone who has touched my life I thank you for making me who I am today. For those who I haven't yet had the pleasure to meet, thank you for entering my world.

Special thanks to my family and most importantly my husband Thomas, who has supported me every step of the way. To my children, who have thrown up cute roadblocks continually, thank you for the inspiration.

# CHAPTER ONE THE MOVE

EVELYN SLEPT FITFULLY, sheets tangled around her legs. She'd been sleeping comfortably until a few minutes earlier, when the dream had started. It was like a movie, even to the extent of having a subtitle at the beginning- *On The Way Home*. Even from inside her slumbering state she'd known it wasn't normal.

Two girls about her age were driving into town. One had long dark hair and was driving with grace, while the passenger had fiery red hair in a messy ponytail. The rest of their features were blurry, as though they weren't fully formed. Evelyn couldn't hear what they were discussing but it seemed mundane, even boring. As she watched, she recognized the set of lights the girls were about to go through on the outskirts of town before everything changed.

A loud crash shattered the night, and Evelyn found herself moving weightlessly through the air. She panicked, until she remembered that she wasn't really there, stuck again in the role of silent observer as she'd been on so many other nights.

Evelyn floated up and above the scene, watching as the girl with dark hair screamed for help, until her voice splintered with exertion and tears. Her hands shook as she fumbled for a cell phone, pulling it out after several frantic attempts. The redhead was deathly white and unmoving inside the car, a trickle of blood from a small cut on her forehead the only motion until Evelyn saw the barest flicker from pale eyelashes as the girl struggled to open her eyes.

Evelyn's attention was drawn to the dark blue mid-size vehicle that had penetrated the side of the car the girls had been driving. The blue

1

car was crumpled just behind the passenger's seat and had narrowly missed the redhead only by inches.

The driver of the other car was slumped over the steering wheel, unmoving, his neck bent at an angle. As Evelyn moved closer, familiarity washed over her. She knew this man, but he felt different, wrong. Whoever it was had been altered, and felt dark and slimy as though already decayed, and missing something important. Before she had time to discover what, she was taken out of the scene, as ambulances arrived, their flashing lights ripping her from the dream.

Opening her eyes to darkness, Evelyn looked over at the clock on the bedside table. Midnight. She felt a shiver coursed down her back and couldn't fall asleep again for the rest of the night. Something was about to happen, something big.

"THIS SUCKS."

Catherine McLean stared morosely out of one of the car's back windows as the pretty but boring landscape moved past her.

"Couldn't we have done this a few weeks ago? Now I'm going to be the big loser who shows up late for school."

Her sister glared at her.

"Oh yeah? How do you think I feel? I had to leave Dave and all my friends. And I'm graduating this year. Way worse. At least you have a few years before you graduate and maybe you'll make some friends this time. I'm probably stuck being a total loner."

Vanessa shot her sister another glare before turning to look out of her own window and muttering something under her breath that sounded suspiciously like 'brat'.

Their mother sighed and turned around to look at both of them.

"Guys, you know this wasn't exactly what we wanted either. But with the economy being what it is, and your dad getting the chance at a better paying job, we just couldn't say no. It may even help enough for us to be able to afford university for you two."

Cat, as Catherine preferred to be called, looked at Vanessa, and silently agreed with her chastised expression. Their parents were trying to make ends meet and the girls could at least cut them some slack about the move, even if it wasn't what they wanted.

Vanessa offered a small smile.

"It's okay Mom. We get it. We're just nervous about the new school situation."

"Yeah Mom, it's fine," Cat added. "It's really great Dad got this job. We'll be good after a bit, it's not like we haven't done this before."

Cat and her mother exchanged genuine smiles, and both parents seemed to relax. The car ride continued afterwards in comfortable silence. Her dad hadn't said anything during the brief exchange, but the set of his shoulders proved that he'd been listening, and Cat was grateful to see his shoulders slacken somewhat. Cat gazed out the window, thinking about the whirl of the previous month. She'd hung with friends at various local hangouts and had been bored. At one point she'd even considered getting a job before school started. Then in the first week of school an unexpected, life changing event had shaken things up.

Her dad was offered a chance to take over as a branch manager at a bank in another town after the previous manager had died. It was a great opportunity for her dad, representing a promotion with more pay, moving expenses,and a house to use for the first year with low rent. Her parents had been struggling to make ends meet and they'd been excited and happy when they told Cat and Vanessa the news.

Vanessa had exploded of course, but she did that over a bad hair day sometimes. This time was legit though, as Vanessa had recently become serious about Dave. Cat was pretty sure they'd gone all the way over the summer. This was supposed to be Vanessa's year; grade twelve, a hot boyfriend, popular. Instead, she was going to be stuck as the new kid with a long distance love and no friends, graduating from a school in which she hadn't even spent a full year.

Cat didn't have it bad in comparison. No boyfriend and just some acquaintances she'd hung with to pass the time. There was nothing and no one super exciting that she'd really miss. They'd only moved a few years earlier from their previous town, and Cat was slow to warm up. Still, it was irritating to be starting all over just one month into the school year. It'd be like walking into late to class late and everyone staring at her, *again*. She hated that kind of attention. It made her skin prickle uncomfortably whenever she was singled out in any way. As a natural redhead, it also meant the prickling usually progressed into a dreadful creeping blush across her fair skin that went all the way up to her pale blue eyes and into her fiery long red hair. She usually ended up feeling like a thin and awkward tomato.

She was okay with her parents having expectations because they were generally pretty low key about things. It was expected that she always try her best but that didn't have to mean straight A's. She did okay academically in general so that wasn't an issue, and when it came to extracurriculars she preferred solitude. In high school she'd dropped out of the team sport circuit and switched her focus to track. It was still competitive but didn't involve team effort or large crowds. She loved the quiet of distance running and found it helped get her through hard times. On a good day she felt as if she was flying, and could sometimes leave the rest of the world behind back on Earth while she stayed far above the noise.

As for friends, it was the same. She was friendly, but didn't share much. It wasn't like she'd had a lot of problems with other kids or people hurting her in her life, she was just slow to trust others. Even with her family she kept a lot inside, but not because she didn't trust them.

It simply didn't seem important to share things when they all had their own issues to deal with, especially Vanessa.

Vanessa had almost the opposite personality to Cat, with her emotions leaking all over the place and getting on everything. Maybe that was partly it. Growing up with her older sister's feelings was as much drama as Cat needed in her life. Cat shook herself out of her reverie and realized that a lot of time had passed during her introspection. The trees and grass outside the window had given way to buildings and street signs again. The town looked nice and had the generic name of Valleyview. It could have been anywhere in North America. She noted a post office, a bowling alley, and at least one movie theatre. They stopped at the bank where her dad would be working at to get the keys to their new house. From the outside, it looked like any other bank in the world. Some brick, some metal, and a whole lot of windows. Cat never understood why banks had so much glass. It really didn't make a place harder to rob, silly buggers.

They drove into the residential area and pulled up on a tree-lined street with sweeping and gracious houses, like southern belles curtsying in colourful ball gowns. The car stopped.

The house looked warm and welcoming, with yellow siding, chocolate coloured shingles and trim. It looked roomy enough so that Cat could have space to herself to sit and think, away from her family and noise. Maybe they could get a cat? She'd always wanted a pet, but they'd moved so often in the previous ten years it hadn't been practical. She watched her dad get out of the car and walk up the sidewalk to the front door. She jumped out, curiosity motivating her to be the first one inside.

She was excited about the possibilities of the move for the first time. The house had a bay window in the upstairs. She'd wanted one since she was a little girl, watching old *Peter Pan* movies in which Wendy told stories while sitting and looking out at the stars.

Her dad gingerly stepped into the house, hand braced on the brass knob as he opened it.

"Hello? Anybody here?"

A cheery looking man with a shiny head of thin red hair popped into view from around a corner like a magic genie.

"Hello! Hello! The McLean's?" The man had a large booming voice, probably aided by his diaphragm being pushed up into his rib cage by a large midsection, Cat thought, stifling a giggle.

"Yes, that's us. I'm Peter, this is Catherine, my youngest, and my wife Mindy and oldest daughter, Vanessa, are coming up the walk. We made better time than I expected, given the couple hundred miles we drove today. The moving trucks will be here soon, I hope."

The other man beamed at them.

"Very good, very good! My name's Joe Dumarche, and I'm one of the realtors in these parts. I had a lady come in and tidy the place up yesterday. It's been empty since the last branch manager...well, since he passed on to glory."

Joe cleared his throat a little uncomfortably.

"He was an older man without any close relatives, but his sister's grandkids cleaned it out for us a month or so back and put it to rights. I hope everything's to your liking!"

Cat thought he appeared slightly anxious, like a guy who truly cared to please people, not like someone just making conversation.

"It looks great so far!" said Cat, feeling bad for him. "Could you show us around a bit?"

Her Dad smiled at her, and squeezed her shoulder. Her mom and Vanessa walked through the doorway and stopped.

"Oh look at the light, Peter!"

Her mom spun around slowly, scanning the open main entry with its high ceiling, stair case climbing the right side and open area to the left leading into a dining area. The main floor had large windows and a good sized stained glass circular window served as the light source near the top of the stairs. Vanessa looked interested despite herself, and Cat could see some of her sister's bad mood ease.

"I'd be delighted to give you the tour," Joe replied, brightly. "Follow me!"

He led them through the house with flair, describing each room poetically. Cat looked at the richly coloured walls and felt her chest warm. The house felt cozy, not cold like she'd feared it might be when she'd first heard that they were moving to an older house.

"Over here is the kitchen."

Joe opened a French door into an oval room, where another door jutted off to the left.

"They used to separate the kitchen from the rest of the house, to keep the servants as far out of sight as possible. You see there's another door here and here."

He pointed to another French door that led to a hall as well as to the back door.

"The basement is through there, over by the back door, but I'll show you the bedrooms first. It's a good size house with four bedrooms for the family, as well as a few other rooms you can use however you'd like."

As they followed Joe, he kept up a stream of conversation about mouldings and details Cat imagined her parents cared about, but she just wanted to get a feel for the place. Sometimes she could tell things about people by how she felt around them. In some cases, she could also get a feeling about objects, especially old ones. So far, even though this house had belonged to a dead guy she felt only warmth, which was a good thing. She'd been scared of seeing ghosts since learning that the previous owner had died in the house, but had tried to shrug off the thought, to avoid jinxing things. Just in case ghosts really existed.

The two rooms on the main floor had pleasant floral patterns for decoration. One had master bedroom written all over it and the other was directly across from it. Not exactly teen friendly. Cat and Vanessa glanced at each other and wrinkled their noses. Joe opened another door Cat had initially assumed was a closet and was surprised to see a small staircase, through which Joe managed to squeeze his girth, while still talking.

"Now this was the servant quarters."

He was puffing a little bit now. They followed him, single file up the stairs. Cat could almost touch the wall on either side with her shoulders, it was so narrow. At the top, the entry way branched into three. A room to the left, which was sunny with a window seat, another to the right with a smaller window and a bathroom tucked into a closet within the room, and a larger bathroom across from the stairs between the two rooms.

"This is an original water closet."

Joe looked proud, pointing to the closet in the bedroom.

"It was just a hole that originally drained down the outside of the house, but my dad, a house builder in these parts, was commissioned to make it into a real room in the late fifties. You won't find anything more solid than a room he was involved in."

Cat's dad took a look around and seemed impressed.

"Do you mind if I call this one?" said Vanessa, as she looked at Cat.

Cat smiled at her, shaking her head.

"Even if I minded I wouldn't say anything. You spend longer in the bathroom than the rest of us combined. You definitely need your own. Besides, I like the window in the other room. I think that looks like a place where I can curl up with a book."

Their parents smiled at each other, and Cat saw them clasp hands briefly.

"Girls," said their dad," why don't you look around a bit more up here while Mr. Dumarche, your mother, and I finish some paperwork?"

He gave them that look parents give when they want you to go away while they speak adult, so Vanessa and Cat nodded and waited for them to leave. They watched as the adults disappeared, before turning to face each other.

"Soooo?" said Vanessa. "What do you think?"

Cat shrugged.

"Looks like a nice house. Rooms are big, and it isn't creeping me out. So far, so good."

While the sisters never openly talked about it, Vanessa knew Cat often had feelings about things, and was more than willing to use this ability to help her make decisions. There'd been more than a few times growing up where they'd escaped from a tight spot because of this knack. Vanessa was dramatic but not stupid and she trusted her sister implicitly. They fought of course, but they were in it together. Sisters first, good or bad.

Vanessa looked around the room.

"Looks like you finally got your bay window, Wendy."

Cat looked at her.

"Ha-ha. That's okay, Cruella. You finally got a makeup room."

Vanessa pretended to pout, dramatically swirling her long black hair while batting her deep blue eyes.

Cat looked around again.

"I wish our furniture was here. I want to unpack, settle in and relax."

Vanessa nodded her head.

"Yeah, staying in a hotel tonight will suck, but at least we don't have to sleep on the floor. And maybe it'll have a pool."

Cat felt hopeful at the idea, as Vanessa looked at her watch.

"Come on, let's see if they're done. I'm hungry."

The girls walked downstairs and found their parents in the kitchen nook, still talking with Joe. They didn't notice the girls at first, but they looked happy. Cat noticed that her mom had that slightly crazy look she got when she thought about painting. The house definitely had enough afternoon light for her mom's hobby.

Her mom had done the stay at home thing for as long as Cat could remember. She'd worked in administration once, but when the girls were born back-to-back life had been busy for many years. She claimed she hadn't enjoyed the work in the first place, and with the cost of child-care being almost the same as her paycheque she decided to stay at home. She'd started to paint again when the girls went back to school and while it wasn't much, it was starting to pay a little. It was also nice for the family to have that linchpin at home. And most importantly, her mom was happy, which made everyone else happy too.

Her dad looked up as he noticed them.

"Hey girls, what do you think? Okay size for the bedrooms? I always thought these old houses had small rooms!"

Cat smiled back.

"Yeah dad, it's great."

"Why don't you girls check out the basement," he suggested. "It's the hallway over there."

He pointed to the back door.

"Stairs are a bit steep, but it's pretty nice. We're just about done here, then we'll go grab a bite before heading to the hotel."

Cat and Vanessa nodded and moved past their parents, while Joe simply twinkled at them. Cat took in the cheery wallpaper as she walked by before descending the stairs to the basement.

While it wasn't a quite a dungeon, it wasn't very exciting either and Cat suspected her dad had been trying to get rid of them. The basement had a plain rec room in basic shades of grey, a truly disgusting bilious green bathroom, and a functional spare bedroom. The rest was open space and a mechanical room containing an old furnace. That room had a bit of creep factor, but just the usual basement level creep, nothing that made Cat feel really uncomfortable.

"Ok my verdict is..."said Cat, pausing dramatically, as Vanessa looked at her. "House seems okay."

"Great," said Vanessa. "One less thing to worry about. Hey, do you think they'll make us go to school on Monday? What if we aren't un-packed?"

Cat laughed at her.

"Of course we have to go to school Monday. You really think mom would let us skip more school than absolutely necessary? You know her, she'd send us as long as we have a change of underwear in the house!"

Vanessa looked dejected.

"Yeah, I know. I was just hoping you'd say she wouldn't. I really don't want to do this."

She plopped down on the carpet.

"It's not like I don't want to get it over with, I'm just not sure I'm ready."

"I know," said Cat, sitting down beside her. "But we may as well get on with it. Hopefully, it won't be as bad as we think. At least we've got the weekend to get settled, maybe walk around town first. I'm pretty sure Mom and Dad will let us go off alone in a place this small. It's supposed to be a safe family town after all."

Cat felt prickling on the back of her neck as she said the words, and her heart sank.

*Oh crap.*

She hoped the feeling didn't mean anything this time, but she was left with a low-grade pit in her stomach that warned her otherwise.

Once they were back in the car, her parents looked as contented as cats with cream. Since no one seemed to care about food other than Vanessa, who was dying of the kind of starvation only burgers could cure, their dad went to the drive through at a fast food burger place, before they went back to the local Super 8. Conversation centred around their mom's gushing about the new house and their dad's frequently expressed joy at the low rent.

"If the job works out and we end up staying, we can choose to buy it or keep renting, since the bank owns it anyways."

"Sweet," Vanessa said around a mouth full of burger. "So far I like it. I just wish we didn't have to deal with the crappy job of unpacking. It's like cleaning, but with all the un-fun-ness of making a mess."

Cat chuckled at her sister.

"Hey, changing the subject, Mom, do you know where the school is? Not to be a keener or anything, but I wouldn't mind driving by and taking a look before we start Monday."

Cat hated the idea of wandering the halls in a strange school trying to find her homeroom. Vanessa gave her a quick thumb and forefinger 'L' to her forehead, to which Cat stuck out her tongue in response.

"Okay there, calm your jets."

Their mom only looked mildly exasperated since she was used to these exchanges between them. She turned her focus to Cat.

"Sure Cat, we can drive by tomorrow and try to take a look. It's the weekend, but maybe they'll be open and you can walk through."

She looked at Vanessa.

"Do you want to come or is that a little too keen for you?"

Vanessa shook her head and shrugged.

"Nah, I'll come. May as well see what I'm in for."

SATURDAY MORNING WAS sunny and breezy, the perfect fall day. They dropped their dad off at the house to wait for the moving van while they went to discover the town. Cat's mom took her time, driving more slowly than she normally would to give them all a chance to look around.

It was a quaint town with a hint of 1950's charm. While it appeared to have the usual stores they needed, they'd all been designed in a traditional wood and brick style, with pastel colours, darker bricks, and large plate glass windows. Wide sidewalks near the stores and planters hanging from the street lights and caged trees on the sidewalks completed the picture. It was very peaceful and quiet as they drove past.

They found the school easily and parked in the visitor's lot. There was only a scattering of cars as expected on a Saturday morning, but the school appeared to be open.

"I want to check the door and maybe walk around. You in, Vanessa?" Cat asked, as she looked at the outside of the school.

Vanessa nodded and leaned over to their mom before getting out.

"Hey Mom, do you mind if Cat and I go for a walk, just the two of us? I kind of don't want it to be obvious that we're here with our mom, if you know what I mean."

Their mom smiled wistfully at the girls.

"Sure, sweetie. You guys go on ahead. I'll fill the car up and come back in a few minutes."

Cat and Vanessa walked around the outside of the school first, looking at the grounds. There wasn't much to see on the high school side. Just an open field with goal posts on either end and trees ringing worn-down grass near the entry way.

Vanessa tried the handle on the door.

"Ready, Freddy?" she asked, grinning as she entered.

Cat followed closely behind. The long hallway before them could have been the mirror image of their previous school, with tile floors and blue lockers lining the walls. *It even kind of smells like my last school. Gross.*

That was one thing she'd been hoping wouldn't transfer with her. The girls skulked down the halls, hoping not to run into anyone or look out of place. They passed what appeared to be the cafeteria, gym, and office, and Cat made a mental note. This is where she would need to be ready to face the music on Monday.

"Seen enough yet?" Vanessa asked, starting to look bored, as she checked her nails.

"Yeah, I'm good. Just have to deal with Monday on Monday I guess."

Cat caught her breath at the thought, a feeling of apprehension curling in her stomach. She'd expected to be nervous about school, but this feeling had an overtone of fear and darkness that that was swift and caused her senses to tingle suddenly like they'd done the night before.

*It feels like something is about to happen, something bad. I just wish I knew what.*

She turned to Vanessa, shaking her head as she walked back out into the sunshine, trying to let it wipe away the dark shadows she could feel collecting in her mind, warning her of oncoming danger.

# CHAPTER TWO
# VALLEYVIEW

CAT GROANED, ROLLING over to the grating sound of her alarm clock swearing at her. She fumbled for the snooze button before moaning in frustration and throwing the clock against the wall. Rubbing her eyes, she rolled out of bed and threw on jeans, a t-shirt, and a hoodie. She paused briefly at the mirror and pulled her long red hair into an acceptable pony tail before heading downstairs for breakfast.

"Good morning sweetie!"

Her mom smiled at her from the sink. Cat grunted hello, before grabbing the fruit loops and plopping down at the breakfast nook. Cat was not now, had never been, and probably wouldn't ever be, a morning person. At best, she was a 10:30 in the morning and onward sort of girl. Which may have accounted for the crap marks in her first class of the day the previous year. She slowly woke up as the sugar made its way into her blood stream.

"Hurry up, dear. You don't want to be late." her mom admonished. "First days are important."

Cat rolled her eyes and looked at her watch, before drinking the rest of her cereal from the bowl. She raced upstairs to brush her teeth and grab her coat. Within a minute the same girl that had been lurching along like the morning edition of the walking dead became The Flash, and was waiting at the front door, ready to go.

"Wow, um, okay....," said Vanessa."What'd you do with my sister?"

Their mother just clicked her tongue at the the girls in exasperation, before grabbing the door and they left, with the girls continuing to grumble lightly at each other.

ONCE AT SCHOOL, CAT's anxiety shot up. Her palms were sweaty and her nerves felt as thought they were encased in ice.

"Are you sure we can go to the office alone? We don't need you to sign anything?"

Her mom smiled reassuringly.

"I can go in with you if you want, but you can bring the admission papers home, too. I know Vanessa would rather I didn't show my 'Mom face' on the first day."

"True," Vanessa said, not the slightest bit ashamed to admit it. "C'mon Cat, let's just do it. Get it over with."

Cat nodded, giving her mom a quick kiss.

"See you after school," said Cat.

Steeling herself for the day with a few deep breaths, she followed her sister into the school.

Cat looked around as they waited in the office. An efficient looking older woman glanced up from a computer.

"May I help you ladies?"

Vanessa handed her the transcripts their mother had given them.

"Um, yeah, we're the McLeans and we're transferring. We were told to come here."

The woman took a minute to look at the papers, then spun around in her wheeled chair, turning her back to the girls briefly while grabbing two folders.

"Here you go!"

She gave one to Vanessa and one to Cat, as she continued chatting informatively.

"This is your schedule and the papers you need for the first semester. You may be able to switch classes later, but as you're showing up into the school year this is all we have at the moment. Catherine, you'll be in

Ms. French's homeroom. Vanessa, you have Mr. Grayson. They are expecting you and will instruct you further. Enjoy your day."

She gave them a brisk smile before turning her attention back to her computer.

Cat and Vanessa walked out of the office and stood to the side of the doorway, watching as the hallway seemed to swell and overflow with students.

"For a small school, it looks pretty busy. Are you ready?" Vanessa whispered to Cat, who grimaced.

The bell rang and the sea of people seemed to part, with kids separating down the hallway into their respective classrooms. The hallways began to empty, so Cat and Vanessa gave each other a quick hug, parting ways towards the rooms that appeared on their schedules.

Cat took another deep breath, looking down the long hallway. At least the rooms had their numbers visible above them. She'd never have found the rooms otherwise. Her classroom was close to the office so she didn't have far to walk. People were still filing into the classroom when she arrived, so she wasn't the last one in. She awkwardly moved past other students, walked up to the teacher and handed over the paper the secretary had given her. Cat waited for direction, feeling the entire room staring at her, as her face began to heat up.

Ms. French was a tall brunette with glasses, pleasant in a nondescript way, who appeared to be around thirty years old. She took a quick look at the papers before smiling at Cat.

"Are you ready for introductions?"

Cat nodded, feeling her breakfast stuck somewhere in the vicinity of her throat.

*God I hate this part!*

"Okay, class, settle down!"

Ms. French's voice rapped the class like knuckles, clear and authoritative. The class quieted down slowly and settled into their desks.

"Everyone, this is Catherine McLean. She'll be joining us this year. Her family has just moved to town. I hope you'll all make her feel welcome."

Cat smiled weakly as everyone continued to watch her. She could feel her face glowing.

Ms. French looked at the class sternly, before turning back to Cat with a bright smile.

"You can grab that seat over there."

Cat saw the chair she was pointing at and walked down the aisle to a seat halfway down the row. A few students smiled at her, a few gave her appraising looks, but for the most part they remained quiet. Ms. French waited for her to sit before turning back to the blackboard.

"Today we'll be discussing quadratic equations."

Cat sighed, pulling out her notebook.

*Great. Now Math will be my worst subject. Mornings suck.*

Classes passed in rapid succession, with Cat continually checking her schedule to make sure she was going to the right room. This meant that other than a few "Hi's" here and there, she hadn't spoken much.

*Small towns are worse than a big city for openness.*

It had been awhile since they'd moved to a town this small, but she vaguely remembered the last time the place had been slow to warm up for her as well.

*Poor Vanessa. This year probably would suck for her.*

She saw Vanessa exit her last class before lunch break and went to join her. Thankfully, they could eat together, today at least. Vanessa probably wouldn't want to be seen with her tomorrow, but on her first day she was as likely to want her sister for company as Cat wanted to be with her.

Vanessa looked around, saw Cat, and came over.

"How goes it?"

"It's okay," Cat replied, shrugging. "Small town. So far I've kept to myself. I find when you're the new kid it's best to wait for others to start talking first. You never know when someone will take offence to a new-bie accidentally talking to a member of the cool group without express permission."

"Yeah, totally. Want to find a place to sit?"

Cat nodded with relief, and they followed the line of students heading to the cafeteria.

Once there, they scanned the room for an available seat. Much like every school cafeteria in the world, it consisted of long tables where different species of students could be found. The obvious jock table, preppies, stoners, nerds etc. They found an empty one and sat down. Cat took out her lunch, surreptitiously checking out people in the vicinity. It was hard being the new kid in a small town when you didn't thrive on attention. You stuck out like an exotic bird without even trying. She recognized a few kids from her recent classes but no faces she could put names to yet.

"So, how'd your morning go?"Cat asked, while opening her sandwich bag.

"Not bad," Vanessa answered around a bite of sandwich. "Seriously. The teachers seem okay so far, and the classes are about where I left off. I'm sure homework will be a bitch for a week or two but otherwise it doesn't seem too bad."

"Anyone talk to you?" Cat asked curiously.

Generally, Vanessa was the outgoing sister in the family, and Cat wondered if the curse of the being the new girl in a small town extended to her as well, or just someone who was introverted like Cat.

"Yeah, I've had a few people make general conversation. Nothing much, but people seem okay. One guy was pretty friendly, but he seems like the kind of guy everyone likes. How about you?"

Cat shook her head.

"Not really," she said, then changed the subject. "I want to find out if they have a cross-country running team, and see if they have try-outs or anything. I may have missed it for the year but want to at least see if it's an option. When we're done eating, do you want to come with me to the office to ask?"

Vanessa shrugged.

"Sure, why not? I still have half an hour until English class starts, and God knows I don't want or need any extracurriculars now. I'm hoping to coast until grad."

While not exactly true about coasting, as her sister was a perfectionist when it came to grades, Vanessa did mean it about sports. They hadn't ever interested her. She was very into drama but the chances of a good drama class in a small town weren't high, so she probably hadn't considered such a class as an option.

The girls finished lunch without any attention from other students, other than an occasional glance. As they walked back to the office, Cat tried to avoid catching anyone's eye, wishing again that she was more outgoing or had a thicker skin. Vanessa stopped abruptly and Cat had to pull up short to avoid running into her.

"Hey, how's the first day working out?"

A boy Cat didn't know smiled at them, and she felt herself colouring involuntarily.

*Damn it!*

"So far so good!" Vanessa chirped.

The boy flashed another smile, and be damned if his hair didn't appear to ripple when he moved. He looked like a movie star with his dark blond hair, dimples and grey eyes. He was probably about six feet tall, slightly taller than Cat, and well built.

He looked directly at Cat and gave another blinding, toothy smile.

"We haven't met, but I guess you must be Catherine. It's not every day we get new students. I'm Declan Boyer, and I'm in History with your sister."

Cat found herself feeling uncomfortable, but not because of his good looks. A weird, cold, and empty sensation came over her. It felt completely out of place in the bright hallway, standing next to a guy who could be a homecoming hero.

"Hey, nice to meet you, too. It's Cat. Um, people call me Cat, generally."

She managed to croak out, wincing at how dumb she must have sounded.

Vanessa immediately noticed she was off, and came to her rescue.

"Hey, Declan, do you know who we'd talk to about a track or running team? Cat was on the team back home before we moved and wants to try out here."

He nodded.

"Of course! You want to talk to Ms. Fisk. She's the Art and Music teacher, but doubles as the cross-country coach. There aren't a lot of teachers here, I mean, the school only has 300 students from grade nine to twelve, so most of the teachers double as coaches."

He looked at his watch.

"I have a few minutes, I can take you to her office."

Cat followed behind Vanessa and Declan, trying to figure out what felt so off. It was more than her usual discomfort with new people. This felt bigger, and she knew she needed to listen to the feeling. It reminded her of the time she'd gone swimming with Vanessa and some of the neighbourhood kids. She'd refused to jump off the dock into the water when she was dared, walking out instead because of a weird feeling she'd had telling her not to do it. The next kid who'd jumped had hit a broken board and torn their leg badly. She had the same cold, dark feeling now that she'd had while wading in the water that day. Something about this beautiful guy made her as scared as she'd been back then.

"And here you go!" said Declan, bowing and waving his arm as though producing a rabbit out of a hat. "Ms. Fisk, in person."

A short and powerfully built Asian woman in her mid-forties smiled at him.

"Oh, Declan, always the charmer!" she said as she fluttered and preened at his attention.

Declan smiled suavely, turning back to Cat.

"I hope you find what you need. I'm on my way to a quick drama club meeting before lunch is over."

Vanessa straightened up, looking interested in something for the first time. Declan noticed and extended the invite to her.

"We're planning the show for the annual spring review. It's going to be a big one this year. We could use more players, if you're interested in joining us."

Vanessa looked at Cat with excitement.

"Do you want to come?"

Cat shook her head.

"You go ahead. I'll be busy here for awhile. I'll meet you outside after school, at the parking lot doors."

Vanessa smiled and gave a quick 'see ya' wave, before turning and following Declan down the hall.

Cat watched them walk away, still feeling an odd sense of unease, and turned to see Ms. Fisk watching Declan walk away with a look of fondness.

Ms. Fisk switched her attention to Cat, giving her a friendly once over.

"So, what brings you here today? Are you a budding artiste, looking for extra work perhaps? A musician? What can I help you with today, my dear?"

Cat smiled, finding the friendly warmth from the teacher relaxing after the oddness that had come from meeting Declan.

"Sorry, no. I'm not the artist in my family. But I'd heard you were the person to talk to about a cross country or distance running club? I was on the track and cross-country team at my last school. I'd like to continue here, unless I missed try-outs or whatever."

Cat felt calm asking the teacher, warming at her open and attentive face.

Ms. Fisk smiled, regretfully.

"Well, the track team is done until spring, but we do have cross-country into November, depending on weather. It isn't a very large group, so there's no need for try-outs. I can introduce you to the other students at the next practice on Wednesday and you can consider yourself officially a part of the team now if you want. The last actual meet is in a couple of weeks."

Cat took down the rest of the information on a corner of a notebook, promising to be at the practice. Maybe she'd get a chance to talk to someone outside of class in an environment she was comfortable in. Feeling more optimistic than before, Cat checked her schedule and headed to her next class, English. Apparently they were learning Shakespeare, according to the titles of her book list. She sighed again, and prayed to whoever listens to high school students.

*Please spare me from a group read along...*

She walked in to find the desks arranged in groups of six and a mad scientist in front of the class. He looked close to retirement age, but seemed to have a massive amount of caffeine in his system. He was conducting some of the other students who had arrived early to rearrange the desks, and when he saw Cat he clapped his hands in delight. "Wonderful, wonderful! Please, come and help. You must be Catherine. I'm Mr. Grayson and this is so exciting! You will be the sixth in this group over here."

He gestured flamboyantly at the empty spot.

"I'm sure you will enjoy the book we are starting today. You have *such* good timing."

Cat felt slightly dazed listening to him. He had a voice like the old cartoon cat Snagglepuss, Einstein's hair, and the energy of a high school cheerleader. Or he was on speed, which would account for everything.

She followed his instructions, moving her desk to join a group of six other students before sitting down. Mr. Grayson turned out to be a force to be reckoned with, exhausting her during her first class with him. He bounced while talking, and was clearly in love with the subject matter. He passed out copies of the book, *A Midsummer Night's Dream,* then assigned them to read and discuss the first act in their groups.

"I want you to remember your groups, because you will be working together until the end of this play."

Cat groaned inwardly. Group project. The two words that created anxiety, despair, and the occasional nightmare. It hardly ever happened that she got people who worked well together. Either she ended up with someone lazy and did all the work herself, or she ended up with a keener who made *her* feel lazy because they wouldn't let her contribute. Either way, she'd had a lot of bad experiences with group projects. She smiled hesitantly at the other students she'd been placed with. The two guys and three girls all smiled back.

One of the girls, clearly used to making decisions, spoke first.

"Okay, let's read the act first, then discuss it. You must be Catherine."

Cat nodded in confirmation.

"Just Cat," she added, quietly

The girl speaking was a short, curvy girl with dark hair and eyes and skin the colour of creamy milk chocolate.

"Great. I'm Evelyn, this is Danae and Melissa."

Evelyn gestured at the two blond girls to her right who looked like a matched set.

"And that's Steve and Robert over there."

Cat smiled again at everyone and they all settled into the chapter to read. After everyone had finished, conversation began in earnest.

The guy with the dark hair, Steve, spoke first.

"Okay, so what do we need to do here? Any specifics on the questions?"

"Yeah, we need to determine who the main characters are and summarize them," Melissa responded and Evelyn nodded in agreement.

"Do we all want to take notes or have one person do it?" asked Robert

"We should all do it, in case Mr. Grayson gives a homework assignment, which you know he will. That way we all have something to work from." Denae responded, with conviction.

"Good point," Evelyn agreed, looking over at Cat. "You've been pretty quiet, do you want to start?"

Cat jumped. She'd hoped they wouldn't ask her anything and looked over the questions Mr. Grayson had written, scrambling to say something intelligent.

"Ummm, okay. A character. Hermia. She's in love with Lysander. Doesn't want to marry Demetrius."

She stopped at that and they all dutifully wrote the name down.

"Hey, does anyone else find this story super confusing? I mean, there's a lot going on."

Denae shrugged.

"It's Shakespeare. He's always confusing. And usually boring."

Melissa nodded emphatically and Evelyn snorted.

"This is nothing! Mr. Grayson loves his Shakespeare. According to a friend of mine who did his class last year, he had three plays assigned because they were 'nice quick reads' that could be finished in a few weeks. He assigns more books than most English teachers because he's manic and thinks everyone else is too."

Cat groaned out loud this time, which made everyone laugh. They continued to work on the project and the class rest of the class passed pleasantly.

After English was over, Cat checked her schedule. She had a spare next then ended the day with gym. Spares apparently were to be done in the library, presumably to encourage the students to read and be quiet. She started off in the direction of library and saw that Evelyn was headed there too. She was walking with some other girls Cat hadn't met yet, but they left and went another direction. Evelyn looked over and saw Cat.

"Hey. Spare?" Evelyn asked, inclining her head toward the library door.

"Yeah. I guess I'll read the play to try to get a grip on what's going on," said Cat, wrinkling her nose at the idea.

Evelyn smiled.

"That's a good plan. Seriously, Mr. Grayson is totally crazy. Knowing him, we probably have two weeks for the whole thing."

Cat shook her head.

"How is it possible someone that old is that energetic? I mean, I'm only sixteen and I'm exhausted just watching him."

"He's psychotic. Friendly and a great teacher, but totally psychotic. At least it's just one class and not the first one of the day. I couldn't handle that in the morning."

Cat agreed.

"I'm not much of a morning person either. I need about two hours to wake up. I used to be good at math, but now that it's the first class of the day I predict a decline in my average this year."

They reached the door of the library. Cat saw traditional wooden tables lined up in long rows, reminding her of an old English schoolhouse. Evelyn headed to a mostly empty one, and looked back at Cat who'd hesitated.

"Well, come on. We may as well sit together if we're going to be suffering through the same English nutter this year."

Cat felt a wave of relief that almost seemed to carry her over to the table.

She put her stuff across from Evelyn.

"Thanks," she said, quietly. "It's a little disorienting coming in to a new school part of the way through a semester."

Evelyn waved away her gratitude.

"No problem. I've been told I can be intimidating, but it's just because I call it like I see it. As long as you can handle brutal honesty we should get along okay. Now, we should probably hush up because the librarian here is a bit of a stickler when it comes to noise."

Cat nodded and started reading, thinking maybe this school wouldn't be so bad after all. Evelyn appeared easy to read, but Cat suspected there was more to her than met the eye. She seemed like the type of person whose bad side you didn't want to meet but who would be a loyal friend until death. Cat didn't get any of the creep feelings from her that she'd experienced from meeting Declan, but was still uneasy.

*Probably because she's more forceful and outgoing I am, but I wonder if it's more than that?*

It wasn't necessarily a bad thing, but time would tell what exactly she was sensing.

WHILE FAR FROM EXCITING, study period gave Cat a chance to figure out where she was in her classes. Evelyn was as proficient at time management as she was at being in charge. They'd passed the entire period quietly reading with an occasional comment on the novel. Otherwise, Evelyn hadn't talked as much as Cat had expected.

*She'll probably end up CEO of some giant corporation in her twenties's.*

She'd appreciated the quiet companionship much more than conversation, as it let her get into her comfort zone with Evelyn more than a gabfest would have done.

Gym class after spare had been a typical one. The teacher had obviously been feeling lazy, so it had been dodge ball the entire time. And now here she was, bored and waiting for Vanessa. And her mom. Again. Sighing, Cat wondered, not for the first time, why she was always the one waiting. She swung her legs idly back and forth on the top of the steps, settling in for a long wait, just as Vanessa came barreling down the stairs.

"Hey, sorry I took so long! I wanted to speak with the drama club teacher before going home. If I want to be involved, Declan said I needed to sign up this week and I didn't want to forget."

Vanessa didn't look at all sorry and instead appeared to be excited.

"They were talking about which play they wanted to do at lunch time and I think they might do *A Midsummer Night's Dream*!"

Cat rolled her eyes.

"You've got to be kidding me! I get to spend English class doing that book *and* they want to do it as their year end play?"

"Yup! It's still my favourite Shakespeare. If you do it right, it's absolutely hilarious on stage."

Vanessa looked around the parking lot, noticing most of the other parents had already gone and the students had cleared out.

"Where do you think Mom is?"

Cat glanced at her watch.

"Give her five minutes. You know she hates crowded parking lots. And she's always at least ten minutes late."

Vanessa shrugged and sat down beside her.

"So, back to the play. They always perform it at the end of the year and it's huge. The whole town shows up, and they use as many people and props as they can. I saw some of the past performances on video and they looked pretty amazing. I was super impressed, especially considering the size of this place."

At this point, Vanessa was almost bouncing with excitement.

"Declan says they always need more people behind stage and try-outs are coming up soon for the main parts."

Cat felt cold when she heard his name, and thought about the oddness of such a reaction. She knew it meant something, but it was so out of place she didn't know what she was supposed to do with the feeling. She almost said something, but just then her mother pulled up in the car and honked the horn. Cat grabbed her stuff, shrugging off the dark feeling that lingered, trying to convince herself it was just new student nerves.

# CHAPTER THREE
# THE TRACK CLUB

THE NEXT FEW DAYS PASSED quickly. Cat was excited for running group and was surprised and happy to see a few familiar faces, including Evelyn and Steven from her English class. The group was small, only about twenty people and very heavy on Y chromosome participants.

Ms. Fisk was no-nonsense, explaining the session briefly, before giving details about the meet the following week.

"Okay, everyone, we have a new member to the group. Cat has been running for several years with her last school, and is going to join us for the end of the season. I know that we only have one more meet, but I'm sure that Cat will be an asset. I've looked at some of her times from last year and I was impressed."

Cat blushed a little, but acknowledged her praise.

"Thanks, Ms. Fisk. I've always liked running. I hope I won't slow anyone down here."

"Now," Ms. Fisk continued, "as I explained earlier, the season is almost over, but that's no reason to slack off now."

She looked sternly at the students.

"I mean all of you. Running doesn't care what anyone else is doing. It's up to each of you to do your very best. The only competition is whether or not you are living up to your previous best and then beating that time."

Ms. Fisk had already warned her the season was nearly over, so Cat was disappointed but not surprised to hear they were almost at the last meet. As she looked at the other students sitting on the grass stretching while the teacher spoke, she saw a few nod and smile at various points. It seemed like this was a familiar speech, and Cat noticed a few students weren't paying attention, until Ms. Fisk stopped to take a breath.

"Practice today will be to run from here to the lake and back. I want to see how well you do with the hills and what it does to your time. You can start as soon as you're ready."

She stopped talking and pulled a clipboard out, writing names down.

The guys took off immediately, racing with each other while Ms. Fisk quickly wrote their starting times down. Cat stood beside the teacher and let her write down the departure time, before leaving with a steady pace. A few of the other girls, including Evelyn, joined her shortly after. While short, Evelyn had an impressively efficient stride and easily kept up with Cat's longer loping gait. They didn't talk much until they finished back at the school, at which time Evelyn grilled her.

"So, what do you think so far?"

She kept walking, cooling down as they neared the school.

Cat looked at her.

"Of what? The running club? School?"

"Everything. Halfway through your first week and no giant missteps so far. I haven't heard much in the way of gossip about you, so that's a good thing."

Evelyn slowed down and then sat, stretching her legs out.

Cat grinned wryly and wrinkled her nose, joining her on the ground.

"Or it could be a bad thing. I'm already so unpopular that no one knows I'm alive?"

"Oh honey, don't you be worrying about that!" said Evelyn, with a look of disbelief.

"You're a tall, athletic, redheaded female. You don't seem crazy, and you have a mysterious quiet thing working for you. Believe me when I say people know you're alive."

Cat felt her ears turn red.

"Um, thanks? I think."

She cleared her throat and answered Evelyn's earlier question, hoping that her face would go back to a normal colour if she changed the subject.

"It's been better than I expected. I'm not the most outgoing person, so I find new schools tough. Unfortunately, it seems like I end up in a new one every few years with my dad's job."

Evelyn looked at her with understanding.

"Oh yeah, I've been there. This is the longest I've lived in one place so far. We moved around a lot when I was younger. My mom's a nurse, and she had to go where the jobs were. My dad died years ago, so it's been just the two of us since then. She's got a good job in town now though, so we've been here four years and I'm good here. People are nice, and it's been pretty chill. Not a lot of drama here, which is both good and bad."

Cat fumbled for words.

"Oh jeez, I'm so sorry to hear about your dad. I really have nothing to complain about in comparison."

Evelyn shook her head.

"I'm not complaining or telling you that to make you feel bad for me. It was a long time ago, and I have a great mom. I just wanted you to know I get that it's hard sometimes."

Cat smiled, and Evelyn smiled back. Cat felt close to her at that moment, the first time she'd felt like that about someone outside her immediate family. It was a strange feeling, but it made her feel a new sense of belonging. And that was a wonderful thing.

They took a break from conversation while they showered then when they were done they walked out together.

"See you tomorrow for more confusing Shakespearian fun!"

Evelyn waved a cheery goodbye and walked over to a waiting vehicle, while Cat got into her dad's car.

"Hey, kiddo," he said. "How was practice?"

Cat strapped into her seat.

"It was good. We have a ten kilometre run next week in Midfield. And I think I may have made a friend."

Cat smiled slowly, more to herself than her dad.

"Are you going to be able to drive me to the meet next Wednesday?"

Her dad thought for a minute, before shaking his head.

"Sorry honey, I have a board meeting that night. Why don't you see if Vanessa wants to take you? You guys can take the car and grab supper on the way home. Some sister time. I know things are challenging with the move, and I really appreciate you guys trying to make it easier for us."

He smiled at her.

"And Vanessa hasn't melted down even once!" Cat shared his conspiratorial grin and they drove home the rest of the short distance in companionable silence.

THE WEEK TOOK ON A comfortable rhythm. Cat and Vanessa spent the weekend alternating between unpacking and catching up on homework, and before Cat knew it, it was the day of the big meet. They headed out immediately after school and when they arrived Cat left Vanessa in the car, playing on her phone while she waited.

"Back in an hour!" Cat called over her shoulder.

Vanessa just waved at her.

"Yeah, yeah. Good luck! I'll be here, unless I have to pee."

And with that resounding encouragement, Cat took off to the starting area. She met up with Evelyn and her other teammates and they warmed up, talking animatedly about the coming run.

They'd just enough time for a short warmup and pep talk before the race started. Cat always enjoyed these events. They usually had a sparse audience, and the only real competition was against yourself, which Ms. Fisk reminded them of during her pep talk, multiple times. It was the perfect sport for a solitary but competitive person. And after she was finished, she could usually get some delicious junk food to fill her belly, which was better than any medal, in her opinion.

As anticipated, it took Cat just under 45 minutes for the run. She made a respectable showing, taking second for the girls with the first place female award going to a local Midfield senior. She was pleased with her time, and figured with more training or a better day she could likely shave another minute off. She said goodbye to the others on the team and walked back to the car.

Evelyn stopped her.

"Hey, hold up!"

She looked worried, with an edge to her voice Cat wasn't expecting to hear.

It was odd to Cat, as she'd never seen Evelyn look anything other than relaxed.

"Sure, what's up? Do you need a ride?"

She could see Evelyn pause, and it almost looked as if she drew a quick breath, before shaking her head and smiling briefly.

"No, my mom's here. I just wanted to, I don't know."

She stopped and shook her head again, clearly bothered by something.

"It's nothing. I'm just stressed about school. Give me a call when you get home? I want to ask you a few things about the play, if you have time later?

Cat shrugged.

"Yeah, sure. I'm just grabbing a bite with Vanessa, but I'll call when we get back. Are you sure everything's okay?"

Evelyn gave her another smile that was probably intended to be reassuring, but failed miserably. Cat didn't think Evelyn could fail at anything. She felt her neck hairs begin to prickle uncomfortably with the feeling of impending doom.

"I'm good. Just drive safe, and call me later, okay?"

Cat nodded, and after promising to call Evelyn again, they parted ways. Cat walked back to the car, still wondering what Evelyn had really wanted to say.

VANESSA WAS EXACTLY where she'd left her, on her phone, with one leg sticking out the car window.

"Hey, how'd it go?"she said, as she sat up lazily when she saw Cat approaching.

"Pretty good. I got second. And now I'm *starving*!" Cat overacted the part of a stranded sailor on a deserted island, while Vanessa laughed.

"Okay there, crazy-face, get in. Do you want to get fast food or go out to a restaurant?"

Cat smelled herself quickly.

"Umm, maybe fast food? I'm pretty ripe and look gross."

Vanessa nodded in agreement.

"You do look gross, but that's not any different than usual."

Cat hit her sister lightly on the arm before doing up her seat belt, then Vanessa put the car into gear and backed out. They found a White Castle a few blocks away and ordered burgers and fries, with a strawberry milkshake for the second place winner.

They pulled over at a nearby park to eat.

"I think I like it here," Vanessa admitted sheepishly. "In Valleyview. I mean, it's only been a week, but people are pretty friendly, they have cool teachers, and I can't wait to get involved with the drama club here."

Cat nodded, surprised, and had to ask.

"What about your friends. Boyfriend?"

Vanessa shrugged.

"I didn't really say much, but I kind of broke up with Dave last week."

Cat nearly choked on her burger.

"What? When did that happen? Why?" Cat heard herself and thought that she sounded like the one in the breakup.

"We decided it wouldn't be fair to each other. Distance is hard, and we both have a lot of things to think about this year. We'll try to keep in touch, but I think it's best this way."

Cat couldn't believe it.

"I thought you guys were really serious though. You know, *serious.*"

Cat looked at her sister meaningfully, and wiggled her eyebrows like Groucho Marx for emphasis.

Vanessa laughed at her.

"Yeah, we were...and I thought he was everything at one point during the summer. But then, well, I don't know. It's like one minute he was perfect, and then I started to see him for what he really was, not what I thought he was or wanted him to be. And he's still a great guy, I mean it. He didn't do anything wrong, but I don't see us together now the way I did before we moved."

Cat nodded her head.

"That makes sense."

"Anyways," Vanessa said, dismissively. "I'm only eighteen and I have a lot to do and see before I settle down for real. I don't see myself married anytime soon and at this point, being single will give me so many more opportunities. I plan on doing a lot of travelling before I set my sights on forever."

She looked back at Cat.

"What about you? What do you want to do after school?"

Cat shook her head slowly.

"I don't know. I haven't thought about it very much yet. I guess university, or take a year off and work, or travel maybe. I'm only in Grade Ten now. I have time to figure it out later."

Vanessa looked at her watch.

"Speaking of time, it's getting late. I told Mom and Dad we'd be back by eight, since it's a school night."

"I'm good to go," Cat said, slurping down the last of her milkshake. "My tummy is happy now."

She leaned back in her seat and rubbed her belly, sticking it out so that she looked about five months pregnant. Vanessa shook her head at her antics, but didn't say anything else before starting the car and putting it in drive.

The trip home wouldn't take long, and Cat was looking out the window thinking about what she needed to do that night. It was Wednesday, and nothing was due before the weekend. She had no tests coming up that she knew of. Probably she'd just shower and read a book, call Evelyn back and wind down before bed.

*It was weird how worried she'd been.*

They'd just started to go through the first set of lights on the outskirts of Valleyview when Cat saw something flash out of the corner of her eye. She turned to get a better look, but screamed instead. Then everything went dark.

# CHAPTER FOUR THE ACCIDENT

CAT BLINKED. SOMETHING warm ran down her face and she couldn't move her arm. People were rushing around her and she could hear Vanessa crying.

"Vanessa..," she whispered weakly.

Darkness and shadows loomed, taking her into their embrace. She closed her eyes again, and faded out of consciousness.

VANESSA SAT NEXT TO her sister, refusing to leave her side while the paramedics and the fire fighters extricated Cat from the car. A police officer took Vanessa's statement, while she sat there in a daze, trying to piece together what had happened. One minute everything had been fine, normal, then the next she'd heard her sister scream and felt the car fold in on itself like a napkin. The police officer, a kind middle aged woman, told her that another driver had run a red light and hit them on the passenger side. They'd been lucky, apparently, because they were hit behind the front passenger door, just behind Cat. Lucky, Vanessa thought bitterly. Had it been any further forward Cat might have been killed. As it was, her door had been bent inwards and they needed to call the firefighters to use the jaws of life to cut Cat out before the paramedics could even attend to her.

All Vanessa could see as she looked around was falling darkness and the flashing of ambulance and police lights. It was actually kind of pretty, she thought, still feeling dazed, as if she was watching a movie. She was numb, and wondered if this was what shock felt like. She hadn't looked at the other car, hadn't been able to, but she could see a white sheet on the ground. Whoever had hit them hadn't been as lucky as they had, and she felt vaguely sad for the other driver.

She managed to call her parents, who understandably were freaking out. Her dad hadn't yet arrived home from his meeting when she'd called, but her mom had said she'd get him and meet Vanessa at the hospital. Vanessa tried to reassure her mom, but couldn't stop crying and knew she hadn't made much sense on the phone. She couldn't get warm or stop shaking, even with all the people who had been there to help them. She felt like she was watching herself act stupid, while her brain was clicking along in a robotic way. It was weird being able to intellectualize what was happening, and still have no control over what her body did.

One of the paramedics came over and gently led her to the ambulance like she was made of glass, fragile and hard, ready to shatter into pieces if dropped. He promised her that Cat was fine, and she would see her as soon as they got to the hospital. She reluctantly let herself be guided to the stretcher, taking a last look over her shoulder at her sister, who was so pale, so bloody. Pieces of glass sparkled like Christmas ornaments in the lights of the emergency vehicles.

And the person she didn't see, covered in a white sheet, who would be a ghost in her dreams for a long, long time. For the first time she could remember, she started to pray. For what, she didn't know.

VANESSA SAT IN THE emergency room, still trembling under the blanket she'd been given by the paramedic. She wasn't entirely sure how it was supposed to keep a person warm, given it was made of silver tin foil, but she held it tight anyways, feeling strangely as if it would keep her safe, like a superhero's cape for protection from the world. The sliding doors opened and her frantic parents burst in, looking around wildly for their daughters. She stood up, and they rushed over. She leaped into her mom's arms and started to cry again, like a baby this time, with deep wracking sobs. Her dad wrapped his arms around her from behind and both her parents squeezed. She winced through her tears, feeling sore places she hadn't realized she had. They let go, but didn't move away.

"What happened? Where's Cat?" her dad asked, still holding onto her hand as he held back his own tears.

Vanessa shook her head.

"I don't know. One minute we were driving, the next someone slammed into us. Then everything was spinning, and there was screaming, and metal and glass breaking. When we finally stopped moving, I realized we were still in the intersection, and a car was stuck in our car."

She stopped and looked at her dad.

"It was *in* our car, Dad. *In our car!*"

Vanessa heard herself shout the words and took a deep, shuddering breath.

"I called 911 and they came so fast I think I was, and still am, in shock."

She laughed, humourlessly, before continuing.

"Cat wouldn't answer me, and she was so white. I did this, Mom."

Vanessa looked at her mom, her lip trembling.

"I hurt Cat. It's my fault."

She buried her head in her mothers shoulder again.

"Shh, shhh," said her mom, as she stroked Vanessa's dark locks. "It's not your fault honey. You didn't do anything wrong. It sounds like you got hit. It was an accident." Her mom continued to hold her while Vanessa cried.

Her dad squeezed her hand and looked around.

"Have you seen a doctor yet?"

Vanessa shook her head.

"Okay, let me go see if I can find someone to talk to. Do you know where they took Cat?"

Vanessa shook her head again, as her dad sighed, brushing her hair off her face before he headed to find someone. Her mom continued to rock and stroke her back, and Vanessa held on tightly while watching as her dad searched for help.

He looked around the room, appearing frustrated and scared from where she sat. He caught sight of a woman sitting at a computer nearby, and headed in that direction. He walked with a stiff and purposeful stride Vanessa knew meant that he was at the edge of his patience.

"Excuse me, I'm looking for Cat McLean, or a doctor that's seen her or my other daughter Vanessa. Or anyone who knows what's going on with my children."

He was trying to sound polite, but Vanessa could hear the strain in his voice and a tone that bordered on rude. The woman, who was obviously used to seeing people at bad moments, gave him a slow once over then looked back at her computer and punched a few keys.

"The doctor on shift today is Dr. Best. She's currently in trauma bay one with a patient. Give me a minute and I'll see if she's able to speak with you."

The woman stood up and walked across the room like she was in glue. Vanessa was positive she was moving faster than she seemed to be, but it still took forever for her to go to a corner room just a few feet away, stick her head behind a curtain, say a few words to someone, then come back.

"She'll be with you in just a minute. If you can please go wait with your family, she'll meet you there."

Her dad came back and sat down with them. Vanessa could tell that her parents were devastated, although they were putting on a brave face. She'd never been this worried about a family member before, and realized at that moment just how lucky she'd been until now. Her family were healthy and happy, and she promised never to take that for granted again, if they only stayed that way.

*If only Cat could be okay.*

ONCE AGAIN, IT TOOK an indescribable amount of time, but finally a small blond woman walked toward them. She was dressed in scrubs and wore a stethoscope around her neck.

"Mr. and Mrs. McLean?"

Her mom and dad both stood, and she gestured for them to sit.

"Please, have a seat. I'm *so* sorry that this has been such a traumatic night for you. I'm Dr. Best. Vanessa, I'd like to take a look at you first, if I may. The paramedics told me that you didn't have any serious injuries, but I wanted to examine you to make sure. Do you have any pain anywhere?"

"Just a little bit from where the seatbelt and air bag hit. Nothing anywhere else really."

Vanessa shrugged her shoulders and winced.

"On second thought, things are starting to hurt a bit now."

Dr. Best smiled professionally back at her.

"Initially you probably didn't feel it, but as you stiffen up, you're going to find several layers of muscle you've never felt before. Any pain in your neck or back?"

As she asked her questions, she gently probed with soft fingers around Vanessa's spine and shoulders. Vanessa shook her head, and the doctor stopped.

"Great. I'm going to give you a prescription for some pain medications and muscle relaxants. You don't need to take them, but I would recommend taking something tonight so you get a good sleep. You'll probably want them tomorrow once you really start to feel your muscles, so I also recommend taking a few days off school and relaxing at home until you feel better. I'll give you a note for school until Monday."

Dr. Best turned back to her parents.

"From what I've heard from the first responders, your girls were very lucky tonight."

She recounted the events of the evening gravely.

"Vanessa had just entered the intersection on a green light, and wasn't going full speed. They were hit by a car that ran a red light while speeding. The driver of that car was pronounced dead at the scene."

Vanessa's mom choked, putting her hand to her mouth to hold back a sob. Vanessa's head dropped down again. It had been a green light. But someone was still dead.

*How could this be happening?*

Dr. Best took a breath, and explained Cat's injuries.

"Cat was fortunate that when the car struck them it hit at the level of her seat, just behind her body. She wasn't hit directly, but the force of the impact caused her to rebound and hit the dash pretty hard. The airbag on her side didn't deploy, but she was wearing her seatbelt, which kept her injuries from being more serious."

She paused to let the information sink in.

Vanessa's dad nodded, and spoke with a quiet and cracked voice.

"Please, continue. What happened to her?"

Dr. Best pulled up a chair, and tented her fingers together on her knees as she sat across from them, before speaking slowly and clearly.

"She has a fractured radius on the right arm and a swollen left ankle, which does not appear to be broken. She has several cracked ribs on her right side, but no underlying injury to the heart, lungs, or abdominal area other than bruising from the seat belt." Dr. Best waited as Mindy covered her face, giving her a moment to regain her composure before continuing.

"She also sustained a head injury, which is the most serious one she has. Her CT scan didn't show any bleeding into the brain, but she does clinically appear to have a fairly severe concussion. She's only been awake briefly since coming to the hospital. She likely will be here for several days, unless that changes soon. We're hopeful that based on the lack of CT findings she will recover fully"

Dr. Best stopped at this point and looked at the family.

"I know it's a lot to take in, but do you have any questions? Is there anything else you'd like to know right now?"

Peter held Mindy when she choked back tears and he nodded.

"Can we see her now? Is...is she able to have visitors?"

The doctor nodded.

"Please be quiet as you come in. Often people with head injuries are very sensitive to noise, but I think she'll want to know you guys are here, even if she doesn't wake up for you."

Peter, Mindy, and Vanessa stood up and followed Dr. Best to the trauma bay.

Cat was there, under the white hospital linen, her skin almost as white as the sheet except for dark purple bruises on her forehead and shoulders. Her red hair spilled messily over the side of her upper arms. Vanessa and her mom both blinked back tears at the sight of her stillness. Her dad went over to Cat's left side and gently grasped her left hand, since the right one was in a cast.

"Hey there, monkey," he whispered, "We're all here, and we're waiting to see you when you wake up." Cat stirred on the bed, and her eyelids flickering briefly, but then her face smoothed and she was gone again. After a brief visit spent staring at her and holding back tears, the family drifted out of the curtained area.

"How long do you think she'll be like that? What should we do?" Peter asked the doctor, in a hushed tone.

"The best thing that you can do, Mr. McLean, is to go home and try to get some rest. I know it sounds awful, but she's comfortable right now and will be watched closely while she's here. The nurses are excellent, and I'll be on call and available all week. If they have any concerns they can call me and I'll come and see her."

Dr. Best lightly patted his shoulder in a gesture of support.

"I don't expect to keep her for very long, but we always like to watch head injuries carefully, and the time frame is unpredictable. Some people are better in a day, others take much longer. You can stay the night if you wish, or you can come back in the morning. Again, she'll be in good hands here. You need your rest, especially Vanessa."

Peter and Mindy debated staying, but Vanessa decided for them.

"I'd like to go home now. I'm really tired, and getting sore. I just want to go to sleep, and maybe this will all be a bad dream tomorrow."

Her dad gave her a comforting hug.

"Okay, honey. Let's go home. Mindy, if you want, pack a bag and you can come back and stay with Cat tonight."

Mindy took a deep breath, wiping her swollen and raw eyes before speaking.

"I'd like that. Okay, Vanessa, let's go home. You and Dad can come back in the morning. Maybe Cat will be awake by then. But like the doctor said, you need rest too."

Vanessa nodded with swallowed tears burning her throat, her eyes still focused on the image of her unmoving sister. They left, each taking a moment to return to the curtained area and give Cat a kiss, casting lingering glances on their way out the door.

Cat slept on, unaware of the world outside.

# CHAPTER FIVE THE HOSPITAL

THE WORLD CONTINUED to spin without Cat's involvement.

After a few hours, she was moved to a private room as the hospital began to wind down for the night. The emergency room had calmed, a lull before the rest of the night, and the nurses efficiently transferred her care to the medical floor. She was whisked unknowingly in a twilight state along grey hallways with florescent lights, smelling of antiseptics and also faintly of bodily fluids. A call bell rang in the distance and infomercials played on a TV in the sitting area by the nursing station. Cat slept on, blissfully unaware of the activity around her. A nurse passed by quietly on her rounds, checking vitals and IV bags, smoothing her sheets before leaving again. Still she slept on. Then she began to dream.

She was walking through the hospital hallways, but everything was different. It was as though a murky dark stain covered each surface, mildewed and foul smelling, as if something long dead and rotting was nearby. The air seemed foggy, or blurred somehow. Through the corner of her eye she saw a rat scurry away, which encouraged her to walk a little faster. Yet the ground was broken, the tile chipped and dented in some places, so she had to pick her steps carefully. She heard water dripping somewhere, both distant and amplified, echoing.

Cat found her heart racing, as she looked for a way out of this grey and scary world. She peered through the doorway of every room, searching for an exit. There was no one around, and no way out that she could see. She was alone. Cat began to feel frantic, hyperventilating with the rising fear of being trapped. She almost cried out for help, until in the next room into which she peered she saw the figure of an ancient woman lying in bed.

*Thank God! A person!*

"Hello?" said Cat, as she cautiously entered the room.

The woman turned her head and looked at her curiously.

"Hello?" Cat asked again, adding, "what's your name?"

Cat inched further into the room, looking around. It seemed cleaner than the other areas, less dank. It was as if the woman herself was emitting a faint, white cleansing glow. She took a moment to assess her, and Cat felt she was looking deep into her soul, then the woman relaxed her intense gaze and smiled.

"My name is Violet. I've been here a long, *long* time and you're the first person who's come to my room. How nice of you to visit. Can you tell me what day it is, dearie?"

Cat thought for a minute.

"Wednesday I think, October 18th."

Violet looked sad.

"So long. I should really get up and do something about this."

Cat looked at her, confused.

"About what?"

Violet sat up in bed and swung her legs over the side. She looked like she was a hundred, but her movements were as quick and light as if she were weightless.

She seemed to float over to Cat, wearing tiny little paper slippers and a gown provided by the hospital that somehow looked like gossamer on her.

She looked up at Cat, coming only up to her shoulder.

"Come," she said. "I want to show you something."

Cat let Violet guide her back into the main hallway and noticed something weird happen as they walked. The air around Violet lightened, and the mildew shrunk back as they passed by. The odd fogginess focused then dissolved around her as she walked. Violet came to a set of steel double doors that Cat didn't remember being there earlier.

"Look," said Violet. "Tell me what you see."

Cat leaned over and looked through the small metal wire reinforced windows typical for the type of door and gasped. There, surrounded by flowers and a few cards, an old woman with white hair lay in bed. Beside her, a middle aged woman was sleeping in a chair.

"What is this?" Cat asked, dumbfounded.

Violet smiled sadly.

"Well dear, that's me. You see, I had a stroke a few months ago. I'm still alive, but as you can see, I'm not all there and I'm not all here."

Cat squinted through the window again and saw the other Violet in the bed open her eyes and look right at her.

"You see dear, we are more than just the sum of parts, A plus B, but we do need both to function completely. When I had my stroke, a part of me split off. My body has been there, waiting, but my soul has escaped incompletely. I am still tied to my body and I need to decide what to do. I can go back, or I can leave. But right now I'm stuck. Much like you."

Cat jerked around, staring at her in horror.

"What do you mean?"

Violet looked wistfully at her.

"Right now, you think you're here, but just as I am, your body is on the other side of a set of doors, waiting for you, for *something*, to happen."

Cat shook her head.

"No, I can't be. I'm only sixteen, I was just at a running meet. I just ate burgers and drove home..."

Cat trailed off, remembering the night's events. She gently touched her arm, her head. She moved her ankle experimentally, realizing that she hadn't felt any of them at all. The areas she could remember hurting mere seconds before she got out of bed were completely fine now.

Violet noticed her movements and smiled again.

"Those injuries you had will not follow you here. They are of the body, and do not touch upon the soul in any way. That remains whole and beautiful, apart. The soul can be injured as well, but not by stroke in my case, or car accident in yours."

Cat looked at her.

"How did you know I was in an accident?"

Violet smiled at her again.

"Why dear, you told me, with your eyes."

Cat was so confused. How was any of this possible? How could a person be in two places at once? And why was this place so dark and creepy? She had so many questions.

"What's going to happen to me? To you?" Cat asked, suddenly realizing that if this woman had had a stroke and wasn't in her body, that could mean she was dying. And if Cat was with her that could mean she was dying as well.

"How do I get back?"

Cat felt her anxiety levels skyrocket at the thought of not making it home.

Violet shook her head and shrugged.

"Ah, that. I've pieced together some information in my time here, and have seen one or two others die on walks through the hospital. I haven't yet seen anyone walk back through the door to the living though. From the few I watched who have gone into the other doors that have opened, there appears to be a choice you make. You need to use all of your energy, without any doubts or reservations, to walk through whatever doorway you chose."

Violet took another look through the door and shook her head again, her face crumpling with regret.

"My body is old, tired and done. I know it's time to move on, but my daughter isn't ready to lose me, and I love her so much. Perhaps that's what holds me here, not of the living and yet not of the departed."

Violet turned to look at Cat again.

"Can you do something for me? A favour?"

Cat was surprised.

"What can I do?"

Violet looked at her daughter with love in her eyes, before turning back to Cat. "When you get back, can you tell Carol that I love her? And she will always be my little girl with the little curl right in the middle of her forehead? And tell her that I'm happy now, and at peace?"

Cat found herself getting choked up and just nodded, not trusting herself to speak. Violet stood up straighter, gazing up at her with a calm acceptance.

"It's time for me now. I'm ready. You'll find your own way in your own time. Nothing can hurt you here, but you must remember that we are all the sum of our parts. When people are missing something, they will be broken and less than human. The soul powers the body and gives us cohesion. Without the soul you are only a shell, a collection of chemical reactions. There is a great evil that wants to collect souls and you need to guard against it. You are special, a firebird."

Violet stoked a lock of Cat's hair.

"You will rise again, and bring renewal, peace, and unity. You have a hard job ahead of you, but remember dear, you have all the power you need, right here."

She placed a faintly perfumed hand on Cat's forehead. She then smiled and backed away, as a door, small and white without windows, appeared behind her. Violet again seemed to float as she moved, and this time when she touched the handle, the door emitted a warm glow. She opened it, and the light warmed the entire hallway. Cat felt the heat warm her from the inside, then Violet was gone, the door vanishing with her in a final blinding flash.

Cat stood still, confused. What had she meant about a firebird? What was all this talk about souls and evil? And how did Violet know anything about her when this was the first time they'd met? Cat's mind whirled with questions, but every time one popped into her head another followed in a crazy train of ideas and concepts she hadn't thought of prior to that night.

She started to walk down the hall, still attempting to figure out what was going on. Obviously she was somewhere outside of the real world. But where? Was this purgatory? It didn't seem bad enough to be Hell, and given she was only sixteen and hadn't done much in her life either good or bad, it was hard to believe that she'd take the express bus there anyway.

The same dank mildewed look she'd first noticed was on everything. It resembled what she imagined the bottom of a lake would look like, if someone removed all the water. She could see more rooms ahead, and walked down the hall toward them. She heard talking and looked hopefully to her left, seeing a small sitting area with a TV. Canned laughter came blaring out of it and Cat was disappointed. She'd hoped it might have been another person to talk to, someone else who could answer her questions.

It looked like a talk show was on, but Cat was struck by the fact some of the people on the show looked dark, while others looked lighter. It wasn't their skin colour, but as if some had a lightbulb inside them, while others had a black light, and the rest were shades and colours in between. The TV also looked out of focus and for a moment Cat wondered if she needed glasses.

As she was puzzling over the TV, she caught sight of something out of the corner of her eye and saw a nurse walk by. She also appeared out of focus, emitting a soft white glow as she went about her work. Cat watched as the woman walked into a patient's room. Unlike Violet, the nurse appeared heavy in her movements.

*Maybe it's me that's out of focus?*

Violet had said that there was the soul and the body. Was Cat was a soul here, with her body behind that door? Is that what Violet had been trying to tell her?

Cat continued to watch as the woman continued her duties. She looked nice, kind of mom-like, with short black hair and caramel skin, and appeared competent and comfortable at her job, performing her tasks with the ease of long practice with soft hands and easy grace. Cat watched her for a while before noticing the patient in the room. She was shocked when she realized it was her! Well, it was her body at least. Somehow, Cat had entered her own room. She looked around, but there was no door like the one that had held Violet on the other side.

Cat went to stand next to herself, and felt as though she had fallen down a rabbit hole. Ha! She thought humourlessly. I'm quite literally beside myself and have no idea what to do. She tried to touch herself, but her hand passed through as if her body wasn't really there. She also noted that, unlike Violet, she wasn't emitting a glow of any kind. In fact, she was quite solid, almost cartoonish. The solidity of the lines around her body was almost as vivid as if she'd been drawn in with a crayon. She watched as the nurse checked her IV pump before washing her face and arms with a cloth, as though she was washing a baby.

"There, cher. That's better."

Cat found the nurse's voice pleasant but it sounded so distant, as if she was talking to her from underwater.

"You're getting better every day. You need to take some time and heal, but don't wait too long to wake up, my little firebird."

Cat looked at the nurse, stunned to hear the same words Violet had said to her spoken by a second person Cat had never met.

"Hey, can you hear me? Why did you call me that?"

Cat tried to talk to her, to ask the nurse what she meant, but the woman didn't hear her. She tried to touch her, put her hand on her hand, but it didn't make contact. It felt briefly warm as it passed through the woman's flesh and it was the same warmth that Cat had felt when Violet opened the door.

*Am I feeling her soul? Definitely something there.*

The nurse moved out of the room, shaking the hand that Cat had touched absentmindedly, and Cat followed. She hoped if she kept following her she might find out what was going on. After all, the nurse had called her firebird and told her not to wait too long to wake up. She must have known Cat was having an out of body, and possibly out of her mind, experience.

*How did she know that?*

As she followed behind, she saw the nurse go into another room containing a different patient. This one appeared to have a glow as well, but it wasn't the soothing, warm glow of Violet and the nurse. This one looked and felt wrong and had the same smell of dankness she was coming to associate with the mildewed hallways.

As Cat watched, the nurse spoke again.

"Oh, Mr. Briggs. You're not a well man. I don't know what you did in your life to get to this stage, but I hope you find some peace before it's too late."

She treated him with the same gentleness she'd given to Cat's body, but was careful too, almost as if she didn't want to catch anything. Cat noted the nurse's glow flicker as she worked, the brightness dimming slightly. The man was sleeping but was obviously unwell.

Cat thought he might have cancer. He was emaciated and his skin was a pale lemon colour underneath it's pallor. Cat hesitated, but was fascinated by the way the nurse had dimmed when she contacted the man. Taking a deep breath, Cat put her hand out to touch the man the same way she'd tried with herself and the nurse.

This time it was different. She didn't feel the nothingness she had when she'd touched herself, but she also didn't feel the warmth she'd experienced when she'd touched the nurse or watched Violet go into the light. Instead, Cat felt cold and damp, combined with an overwhelming sense of darkness. Pulling her hand away in disgust, she observed that it seemed dirty. The stain faded rapidly, almost as soon as she noticed it.

She looked at the man in confusion. He seemed a shade lighter than he had before she'd touched him. She tried again, and this time held her breath, trying to push past the feeling of revulsion. Now when she took her hand away it was black, as though she had stuck it into a muddy hole. As she watched, the man the nurse had called Mr. Briggs continued to lighten all over and the darkness on her hand faded back to normal. This time she was left exhausted, and collapsed into a chair in the corner of the room. It felt exactly like she'd just finished a long run and was starting to stiffen up before stretching. As she rested, the feeling slowly abated. The nurse had left to get something during Cat's experiment and returned at that moment, gasping in shock.

"Mr. Briggs! What did you do?"

But the man continued to sleep, unaware and uncaring about being interrogated by a short woman who sounded more and more like an angry mother hen, as she clucked around him.

Suddenly, the nurse stopped talking. She appeared to be sniffing the air for a few moments before she spoke again.

"Something is different here. There is a presence and I sense a change."

She looked suspiciously around the room, stopping when she caught sight of the chair where Cat was recovering. The nurse looked at the chair intensely, as if she could see Cat, trying to catch her breath.

*Maybe she can see me?*

"Hello from the other side?" Cat said, hopefully.

Disappointed, the nurse shook her head.

"I could swear something is different here, but I can't see it. My eyes are failing me today. Ma Grand-mere would be so disappointed!"

She tidied up her work area, mumbling to herself under her breath and shaking her head, then left the room when she was finished.

Cat took a last look at the man in the bed. While not exactly glowing white as the others had been, she could see he was now much a lighter shade, and appeared to be sleeping peacefully. She stood, thankful that some of her exhaustion had passed. She started to leave the room but stopped when she heard a man speak.

"Thank you."

At first, she wondered if she'd imagined it, but when she looked back at the bed she could see his eyes were open and he was looking right at her, not though her.

*He didn't look well. Like he could die any second, and maybe would.*

"Were you talking to me?" Cat asked him, curious as to why he could see her when the nurse couldn't.

"Yes. Thank you. I feel more like myself again," he said, smiling crookedly. "Well, like myself with pancreatic cancer. But inside..."

The man paused thoughtfully.

"I feel whole again inside. For so long I've been tortured by what I've done with my life..."

He stopped again, closing his eyes and almost appeared to have gone back to sleep before he surprised her by opening them again and speaking.

"But now I'm free....and I'm ready."

Cat blinked.

"Ready for what?"

She was starting to get nervous when people said that.

He smiled weakly at her.

"I'm ready to go. The next adventure, right? I didn't even know what I was holding on for. But now I think it was for this, to feel complete again."

As Cat watched, he seemed to become brighter, the glow around him changing to the same bright colour she'd seen around the nurse. Then he closed his eyes, this time going back to sleep.

Cat felt like Alice in Wonderland must have done, completely disoriented and discombobulated. Figuring she wasn't going to get any more answers in the room, Cat again entered the disgusting hallway. She didn't see the nurse anywhere, so she kept walking, hoping to see something that would help her figure out what was going on. More importantly, anything that would let her get back into her body. She thought again about the wave of exhaustion that had run through her when she accidentally took the darkness from the man back in the room. But now she felt fine again, which was weird.

Cat arrived at another room and looked in. She saw a different nurse giving a patient medications. Both of them had a steady, light glow in different shades of gold and silver, which for some reason Cat thought appeared healthy. She wasn't sure why that thought came to her, but when she examined it, it felt right. They seemed like healthy colours, not sick like the ones in Mr. Briggs' aura. Cat walked on, continuing to look for a door. She cautiously peeked into another room, and saw another old woman staring mutely at the wall. Cat could see a darkness hovering around her, and this time wanted to see if she could remove it. Firming her resolve, Cat entered the the room and walked over to her.

"Hello," Cat said, not expecting a response.

This time, the woman in the bed turned to her with fear in her eyes. She didn't speak out loud, but Cat could hear the woman's voice inside her mind.

"Am I dead? Are you here to take me away?" the woman asked with a tremor.

Cat shook her head.

"No. I want to see if I can help you. You're surrounded by darkness, can you feel it?"

The woman's eyes widened.

"You can see it? I've been different for about a year now, since my dog died. I was out walking him and someone, I don't know who, a boy, bumped into me. I could feel my dog panic, then he bolted. I saw him get hit by a car and I felt a deep wave of darkness wash over me. I don't remember what happened next, but when I woke up, they told me I'd had a stroke, and that was why I couldn't remember things. Why I lost my words and have weakness in my body. I can't get better, and I've been stuck in this body, feeling this darkness inside me ever since."

The woman implored Cat with her eyes, voice pleading in her head.

"Please can you make this suffering end? I can't live this way any longer. I'm not me."

Cat remembered what Violet had said about body and soul being more than just the sum of parts. About how if one part was missing, a person would be broken and less than human. But what if one was missing only *some* of one's soul? Could that do what this woman was describing? Make people think she'd had a stroke? What could do that to someone? At this terrifying idea, Cat hardened her resolve to at least try to help her. Maybe that's what Violet had meant when she'd said there was a great evil that wanted to collect souls. If she really was this firebird thing, and it was her job to bring peace and unity, first she needed to learn how to do it. With Mr. Briggs she felt she'd done something already, but she needed to know it hadn't been a fluke.

Cat leaned over the woman.

"Just relax, and I'll try to remove the darkness I see."

The woman closed her eyes, and waited. Cat leaned in, this time instead of using just one hand, she placed both hands on the woman, one on her head and one on her heart. It seemed right somehow, fitting that a soul would need both brain and heart to be correctly seated in someone. As she touched the woman, dark water flowed into her hands and her body. She was struck by the sensation that she'd jumped into an ice cold glacier lake and the water covered her head, drowning her under it's weight. She gasped, releasing her hands from the woman and felt as if she'd bobbed back to the surface after just swimming a mile.

She crumpled to the floor and leaned back on the wall, breathing rapidly. After what could have been a few minutes or a million years, Cat was able to stand up. She got to her feet slowly, waiting to see if she felt any residual weakness. Cautiously she ran through a body check and realized that she felt normal again, although more tired than before.

Cat looked at the old woman again and this time saw her shining so brightly she could hardly keep her eyes open from the glare. Brighter than the nurse, even brighter than Violet had been. The glow dimmed as Cat watched, but remained a brilliant white, with no trace of the darkness she'd first seen.

"You did it!"

Her face broke into a smile and she moved cautiously in the bed. She got up slowly, placing her feet in fuzzy pink slippers and walking with a testing gait towards the door, looking back over her shoulder at Cat with gratitude.

"I can't ever thank you enough. I don't know how, but know you are blessed, and thanks to you, I'm saved! I'm whole again!"

She walked towards the door to the hallway and a passing nurse gasped.

"Oh, my God! Dorothy! You're out of bed?"

Dorothy smiled at the woman.

"Yes dear, and I think I feel ready to go home now. Do you know if I can?"

The nurse stood there, her mouth agape.

" Um...I...um, let me call the doctor, okay? He'll have to see you before you can leave and it won't be until tomorrow at the earliest."

She stared at Dorothy with suspicion.

"I didn't know you could walk. And I've never heard you talk before."

Dorothy waved her hand dismissively at the nurse.

"I've never had much to say to you before."

Cat was stunned. In this place where she was a spirit or soul, or whatever she was, she appeared to be able to touch the souls of other people. In her own case, she couldn't do that because she wasn't physically there. It was starting to make sense, but would this extend to her own body? She'd yet to figure out how to get to herself.

I hope there isn't a time limit, she thought uneasily, remembering how the nurse had warned her to get back to her body as soon as she could.

Walking down the hallway again, Cat thought about what Violet had done. There had been a metal door and a white door. She'd chosen to go through the white door. Maybe if Cat went back to the room where she'd last seen her body, she'd be able to find a metal door that would open for her. If Violet had gone through the white door and into the light that meant the metal door was the one Cat needed to find to get back home.

*At least it's a starting point.*

Cat changed directions and headed back the way she had come. She noticed that some of the mildew in the halls had receded from outside the rooms of the two people that she'd healed.

*Maybe the reason for the darkness in the building is the darkness in the souls within it*, she thought as she walked.

So many maybes, but no way to know for sure. She once again passed the sitting area with the TV then at last came to her room.

This time instead of focusing on how odd it was to see herself in bed, she looked around the room, trying to really see all it. While it didn't appear to have mildew like the halls had, it was every bit as dark. It seemed empty, a neutral dark grey instead of light or dark like the other rooms she'd seen. She stood in the doorway, slowly turning around, looking at every detail she could make out. This time, she saw a big metal door opposite the entrance where she'd come in, across from the sitting area. She walked over and looked through the same metal lined windows through which she'd seen Violet's body through earlier. And there she was.

Cat looked at herself through the window and could see the cast and the bandages. Her head was almost purple on one side from bruising and she was even paler than usual, her redhead complexion now bone white instead of fair. Looking at herself from elsewhere was disorienting, knowing it was her body, yet being detached from it.

Remembering what Violet said about needing to want the change with her entire being, Cat concentrated on the door, trying to shake the sensation of being lost and alone. At first, she tried to open it with her hands. Nothing happened and she began to get scared.

*What if I don't make it back to my family? I'm too young to die! But I can't stay here forever either.*

She took a deep breath to calm herself and used all of her willpower. Instead of pulling, she turned the handle, believing it would move with everything she had in her.

And then she walked through into the light.

# CHAPTER SIX THE CONVALESCENCE

CAT GASPED AND SAT up in bed. Her heart racing, she touched her chest, her arms, her head. She could feel herself, she was solid.

*Ow!*

She realized that, although happy she was solid, she could now also feel every single bruise she'd seen while looking at herself through the glass. She touched the bed beside her then saw the call bell and hit the button. She needed to talk to someone, anyone. She needed to know she was real, that she was still alive, and that meant she needed a real human interaction to confirm her existence.

*Maybe it had all been a dream. Maybe none of it was real.*

Hopeful that she'd merely had a bad dream, Cat rationalized everything she remembered seeing and doing before waking up. After a few minutes of self-talk and convincing herself it had only been a bad dream, she felt better. Until the nurse walked in.

It was the same nurse who'd been talking to her in her dream. Or was it an alternate reality?

"Well hello, cher! So good to see you awake. There are some people who will be very excited to see you are back among the living!"

Cat looked at her.

"I remember you."

The nurse smiled at her, eyes sparkling with humour.

"Well, my name is Marie-Jean, and I've been your nurse tonight and for the last few nights. So, I hope I look familiar!"

She chuckled a little before continuing.

"Your parents just went home to get a bite, but I'll call them. They've been waiting a long time for you to wake up, mon petite chou."

Cat looked around for a calendar, but didn't see one.

"What day is it?" she asked, apprehensively.

Marie-Jean smiled at her.

"Well, it's time for you to get candy! Tonight is Halloween."

Cat stared at her in astonishment. That meant that she'd been asleep for thirteen entire days. It had felt like hours.

*My parents!*

"Can you call them right now? They must be terrified for me."

Marie-Jean smiled and patted her hand.

"Of course, right away."

True to her word, Marie-Jean left the room, returning only minutes later.

"They're on their way over. They were so happy to hear you're awake they almost dropped the phone. I also called the doctor. She'll need to see this as well."

Cat closed her eyes. It was all too much. How could she have been unconscious for thirteen days? It seemed like something out of a movie, a bad sci-fi one that comes on after infomercials, just before the TV goes dead. She suddenly felt tired and thought how silly that was, given that she'd apparently had a two week beauty sleep. She turned her head and opened her eyes again, looking out the window.

She saw a tree with leaves gently rustling in the wind. She watched it in appreciation of its beauty and found herself mesmerized by the tree's simplicity and elegance. She fell into watching the dance of the leaves. Marie-Jean left at some point while she was captivated and Cat appreciated the silence, even though she also wanted company.

It felt like only seconds had passed before she heard a gasp and a woman crying. She turned her head just as a female projectile with long hair landed gently on the bed next to her.

"Hey," Cat said quietly, her voice cracking from disuse and emotion.

Her sister gave her a gentle hug, crying.

"Oh Cat, you scared me so bad! I haven't been able to sleep since the accident. I couldn't stop worrying about you. I'm so, *so* sorry!"

Vanessa looked at her, eyes swimming with tears.

"I guess I've been sleeping for you," Cat joked weakly, and her sister punched her arm, more gently than she usually would have.

"Ha, ha, so funny. And here I thought your attitude would improve with a nice long nap."

Vanessa stuck her tongue out at her sister, her wet eyes confirming to Cat how much she'd worried. Her dad cleared his throat behind them.

"Hey, Dad," said Cat. "I missed you guys. I've had some crazy dreams in the last little while that you just wouldn't believe."

Cat smiled at sight of her parents, her mom standing next to her dad, smiling with tears streaming down her face. Both of her parents came over and touched her lightly on her shoulder and arm, but it was her dad who asked the question.

"Hey, honey. How are you feeling?"

"Not too bad, really. My arm's a little sore, but my head feel's okay. I guess I just needed to rest?"

He kissed the top of her head.

"You really had us worried there for awhile. I'm glad to see you awake."

Cat smiled.

"Yeah Dad, me too. Do you think they'll let me go home tomorrow?"

Her dad shook his head.

"I'm guessing waking up after nearly two weeks may earn you a few more days in hospital, sweetie. We'll have to wait and see what the doctor says."

Cat nodded.

"Yeah, I figured as much. I just miss my own bed. I'm strangely tired lately."

She smiled again, and found her eyes getting heavy.

"Okay, Cat," said her mom, as she spoke for the first time that day. "Get some sleep, real sleep, now. I'll be back first thing tomorrow. I'll even bring you some cinnamon buns for breakfast from Starbucks."

She winked at Cat.

"The food here is awful. Trust me."

THE NEXT MORNING, CAT stretched herself awake, enjoying the sensation of cool sheets under her heels, feeling the muscles in her arms and legs protesting after the lack of moment, enjoying the movement of taking a deep breath. She even found the pain from moving her arm invigorating. She'd never realized how amazing it was to be able to move before she'd been outside her body and unable to appreciate it. She caught herself staring out the open window again, feeling the breeze caress her face. Today she could see a small bird's nest in the crook of the tree, with babies peeping for food. The mother bird flew in as she watched and she could see a faint shimmer of white around it as it dropped a worm into the nest. Cat squinted at it. Yes, there was a faint glow. Maybe her dreams *were* real after all.

She heard a knock on the door and carefully turned her head. It was the doctor she remembered from the ER, when she'd briefly woken after the accident.

"Hello, and nice to finally meet you!"

Dr. Best gave her a smile and took a clipboard off the end of the bed. She quickly scanned it, then looked back at Cat attentively.

"So, how are you feeling today? I must say, you look a lot more lively than the last time I saw you."

Cat smiled.

"I feel alright. My arm's sore, but my head feels a little better today."

Dr. Best nodded.

"That's good. I want to run a few more tests, but if you do well over the next few days you should be able to go home. You'll need to get a lot of rest, and you'll be more tired than usual. Head injuries are a big deal, even when nothing is broken and we have normal imaging. The fact that you were out of consciousness for this long means it will take you longer to get back to normal, although your age will help with recovery."

Cat nodded. While she was eager to leave, she wasn't going to be stupid about it either.

"I'll do whatever you recommend. I can't wait to get home, but you're the doctor."

Dr. Best smiled at her.

"That's true, but you're the best person to know how you feel. You'll have to take it easy with sports and other things that could aggravate it, including school work, for awhile. You have had a serious concussion and that's nothing to take lightly."

Dr. Best explained a few things she'd have to watch for over the coming days, but left after a few more minutes, leaving Cat alone with her thoughts again.

The next few days passed quickly in hospital. As part of planning for her to go home, Cat was assessed by a physiotherapist, an occupational therapist, several nursing and medical students, and various other groups of people she lost track of. She had another CT scan and more blood work before it was finally decided she was well enough to go home. She'd have to follow up with both the head injury clinic as well as Dr. Best to have her cast removed in two weeks for her fracture to be reassessed.

She was also under strict orders to stay home and not do anything more strenuous than gentle walks until her headaches were gone. Cat didn't mind the order at the moment. She still had a headache all day, every day, and hurt all over, but she knew that she'd be tired of resting in short order. She was a high activity person, so staying away from running would be tough.

*Hmm, I wonder if I can run wearing a cast. I bet it would be awkward. Oh well, it's only a few weeks. At least I'm alive and healing.*

Her mom entered the room, and this time had brought banana bread. The cinnamon buns the previous day had been good, but sadly her mom had been right about the quality of the hospital food. Cat ate hungrily before packing her few belongings and happily leaving the room behind her without a backward glance. They walked through the hallway past the nurses station, where her mom dropped off banana bread and a thank you card for the care Cat had received, before they continued on.

As they walked, Cat looked around to see if she could catch any glowing like what she'd seen in her dreams, or even the faint glow she thought she'd seen around the birds nest, but saw nothing to confirm her theory. She tried with everyone they passed, but remained disappointed. Nothing. Just regular people and boring hallways.

*Maybe I did dream it.*

Frustrated but happy to be free, she walked out into the sunshine with her mom, escaping the place where she'd been trapped for two long weeks.

THE NEXT FEW DAYS PASSED as slow as molasses. Now that she was out of the hospital, Cat was impatient to be better already. Instead, she found herself physically hampered by her cast as well as by a constant, low grade headache. It made concentration difficult, and made her feel clumsy when speaking and slower with her thinking. She found that she got upset easily, and often felt like crying over things that were trivial and usually wouldn't bother her. It made her wonder at times, in her more bitter moments, if Vanessa had been dropped on her head at birth and that's why she was so dramatic.

She'd never had a concussion before, and hadn't expected it to be so hard to deal with. It was her brain, but it wouldn't do what she wanted. She couldn't watch TV or go on the computer and she couldn't focus on reading for more than a few minutes at a time without her headache getting worse. She felt as if all she could do was lay in her bed like a useless lump, which made her more frustrated than she could handle.

Dr. Best had reassured Cat and her parents that she expected a full recovery based on the clinical picture, but she'd also warned them to expect that it would take time until she felt better, maybe even months. Dr. Best said she would follow Cat's recovery and while she liked the doctor, Cat was hoping she wouldn't have to see her for very long. She was already chafing at the imposed restrictions, and the idea of it taking months to get better made her feel like screaming. Initially, she'd been mad about the order to stay home for a full week, but now that she was having so many headaches she was worried she wouldn't be able to handle going back to school.

*What if the headaches don't get better?*

Cat spent a lot of time in her room, enjoying her bay window, staring down at the tree lined street below. She found it hard to concentrate on the homework that Vanessa brought home from school, but kept working through it a page at a time and mostly succeeded in finishing it by the end of each day. As the days passed, she slowly found it easier to concentrate. There were even brief headache-free intervals, although not nearly as many as she would have liked.

She walked every day to rebuild her atrophied muscles. She itched to run again, both physically and mentally, and it pained her that she wasn't able to. She was having running withdrawal, but kept to the recommended pace, simply because of her inability to move any faster. The weather was now getting colder and she often came in from her walk with her nose pleasantly tingling. She'd then have an Epsom salt bath to warm up her sore muscles, with her arm in a garbage bag to protect it from the water.

The only good thing about being unconscious for so long was the time it would take to get her cast off. She had another appointment that week for X-rays and depending on how she'd healed, it might be time to have the cast removed. It had only been a hairline fracture, and it was almost four weeks now since the accident, so she was hopeful. Maybe she'd be able to start running afterward, if her head cooperated.

Cat heard her mother calling, and uncurled from her perch by the window. She took a last look around her room as she turned off the light, feeling a burst of happiness. Spending time being still wasn't easy, especially right now while restricted by her healing body. She felt as though she'd finally nested somewhere, forced into it by her convalescence. She felt at home, in this town, in this house. A warmth spread within her chest and a tingle fanned out, travelling all the way to the tips of her fingertips like electricity running along wiring.

As she walked downstairs she continued to feel tingles, noticing her headache had faded. Simultaneously, she realized her wrist felt good. Still stiff from being immobilized in the cast, as though someone had wrapped it in cotton for no reason, but without the ache that had been present just a moment before. She wondered if the two things were related, but put the thought aside to mull over later when she saw her mom standing precariously on the kitchen counter.

"Woah, Mom, what are you doing?"

She hurried into the kitchen, putting her good hand out reflexively to keep her mom from falling.

She was standing with one leg on the counter, and the other floating behind her for balance, while her upper body had vanished into an empty cupboard. She turned her head slightly to look at Cat, maintaining her grip easily.

"There you are! I'm just giving everything a thorough clean. I know Mr. Dumarche said he'd had a cleaner in, but they never get the out of the way areas. Now things have calmed down a bit, I thought it was a good time to do a deep clean before we start Christmas preparations."

Cat blinked at her.

"Christmas? It's hardly even the end of November."

Her mom made a snorting noise and gave the inside of the cupboard another swipe with her cloth.

"Time goes fast, sweetie. Now, you need to be ready to go in a few minutes."

Cat looked at her, confused.

"Go where?"

Her mom looked at her with a chiding glance before giving the cupboard another sweep with the cloth.

"Why, your doctor's appointment of course. We're seeing Dr. Best at the hospital today."

"Today? The hospital?"

Cat could have sworn the appointment was tomorrow.

"Yes, the office called this morning. Apparently, Dr. Best was called in to cover ER today and tomorrow for another doctor, and her clinic had to be cancelled. They said you can come in today, as mornings during the week are slow, get your repeat X-ray through emerg, and she'll see you afterward."

Cat nodded.

"Okay, that makes sense. I thought my memory was getting worse instead of better! I'll get dressed and then I'll be ready."

Her mother smiled.

"I'll be here. I'm done with the cleaning, so I just have to put away the dishes. If we have enough time after we're done at the hospital and you feel up for it, we can grab lunch as well."

Cat gave her mom a salute with her cast, marvelling at the lack of pain, and went upstairs to change.

Clothing was still a struggle, since her usual choice of jeans, t-shirts, and hoodies weren't cast-friendly. She continued to gingerly move her cast arm around, feeling the absence of pain, as though a magic wand had removed it. It had disappeared completely, at the exact moment she'd felt warm with happiness. Maybe it was related to the feeling she'd had with the tingling? Her headache was gone, but it had already started to come and go instead of being there full time before that, so maybe it was nothing. Maybe Dr. Best would give her permission to return to school on Monday. She'd missed so much school right after getting caught up from the move. She didn't want to miss more than she needed to and now that she felt well, maybe she'd be able to return right away. Also, she'd now be the new kid that almost died. For someone who didn't want attention, she was sure doing all the right things to get it.

*The sooner things get back to normal the better.*

The ride to the hospital was short. They registered at admitting and were given a sheet of paper to take to the X-ray department. Cat went through the motions as directed by the X-ray technician, and when the procedure was finished they were told to have a seat back in the waiting room. Cat looked around, noticing a few people in varying stages of infectious illnesses. She made a mental note to wash her hands well and not touch her face until after they left. She didn't need a cold on top of everything else. The TV was playing a talk show she didn't recognize, and the room was decorated in several different shades of beige. A man went by on an automatic floor cleaner and briefly Cat thought it would be fun to try driving one. Her random thoughts were interrupted by someone announcing her name, so she stood and went over to the ER doors, where a nurse was waiting with a clipboard.

The nurse took her vitals, asked a few questions then whisked Cat and her mom into a bay with a privacy curtain, where she instructed them to wait. Cat prayed she could get the cast off. Now that her wrist didn't hurt anymore, she wondered if it was healed. *Could that be part of the firebird thing Violet had mentioned?*

The details of her dream were intermittently sharp and fuzzy. She called it a dream because she'd been 'asleep', although maybe calling it an out of body experience would be more accurate. She wasn't sure if it had really happened though, so dream was a better fit in her mind. Maybe if she researched at home what a firebird was, she could find some answers for the questions swirling in her head.

"Hello, Catherine!"

A sunny voice and smiling face accompanied the words as they penetrated into Cat's mental dialogue. She looked up and saw Dr. Best holding a chart, looking at her. "How are you feeling this week? Any improvement?"

"Actually, I feel completely back to normal today," Cat replied, surprising both her mom and the doctor.

Her mom smiled and patted her hand.

"That's great, honey!"

Dr. Best wrote something on Cat's chart while nodding.

"How've the headaches been? Are they there at rest or just with activity?"

Cat shook her head, marvelling at how normal it felt with movement now. "They've been slowly getting better, and today they seemed to disappear completely. I haven't had one at all since breakfast. And my arm doesn't hurt either."

Dr. Best looked pleased.

"Well, your X-ray looks good to me, but I'm going to run it by our radiologist to double check. If they agree, we'll take the cast off and give your arm a test-drive."

Cat smiled, excited to be improving. She felt the same warmth as before bloom in her chest, and as she looked at Dr. Best, she noticed a faint shimmer around her, almost gold in colour and warm like her hair. She gasped, but managed to choke back the noise. She looked at her mom and her breath caught again. Her mom's head was also sur-rounded by a shimmery light, but hers was more silvery in nature.

Cat felt the warmth fade as her astonishment grew and as it retreat-ed, so did the light around the two women.

*Maybe the glowing feeling was connected to seeing the glowing?*

Thinking back to when she'd been in the hospital and had seen the bird in the tree, she'd felt warm and happy then as well. That was the last time though, as she'd been in a perpetual state of discomfort until today. She'd been glad to be alive and leaving the hospital, but not hap-py in the true sense of the word. Today was the first time she'd felt felt that warmth and happiness since watching the birds. At the exact mo-ment she'd felt the warmth, her pain had vanished. Violet had said her gift was regeneration and healing. Had she healed herself?

Cat absently noted Dr. Best leaving. She kept reexamining her memories, but it was only a few minutes before Dr. Best returned, in-terrupting her attempt at piecing things together.

"Great news!" said Dr. Best."Dr. Guidache, the radiologist, believes your arm looks fully healed on X-ray. That means we can take the cast off and you can start doing physiotherapy to regain your strength."

Cat gave her mom a hug, which was returned with gusto.

"This calls for a celebration!" said her mom, beaming.

Dr. Best smiled, clearly happy to see Cat improving.

"Do you feel like you're ready to try going to school next week?"

"I'm ready. I'm super bored at home, so I may as well bite the bullet and go back now. I'm already behind, and I'd like to try to get caught up before Christmas break, if possible."

Dr. Best nodded, and wrote her a note.

"Just take it slow, and make sure that if you have any set backs, you decrease your activity until you feel better. I'd like to see you again in three to four weeks to see how it's going, but I see no reason why you can't go to school Monday."

Cat smiled again, thanking Dr. Best and taking the note. It felt like she was finally getting back to normal. If being a firebird, whatever that was, was normal.

CAT AND HER MOM WENT to a nearby family restaurant for lunch. Her mom looked happy, more so than Cat had seen her all week. Cat was happy too, but thought it would probably take another week of showers until her arm smelled normal. The area that had been under the cast was thinner, as expected, but Cat had not been prepared for what skin that had been under a cast for a month looked and smelled like. Gross. Talk about zombies or mummies. Wear a cast for awhile and you too can have the makeup free version. Her arm smelled like death.

"It's been a rough few weeks, Cat," her mom said seriously, taking Cat by surprise.

"Yeah, I guess so," she replied, not sure where her mom was going with her train of thought.

"I love you and your sister so much. When we got the phone call, well, it was tough on me and your dad. And then to see you lying in that bed so pale, for so long, not talking to us... I've never been through anything so hard. Even when your Gramps died, I was expecting it be-cause he was so old. But you, Cat," her mom's voice broke. "I thought I was going to lose my baby."

She blinked back tears.

"I just wanted you to know that no matter what, we love you fur-ther than the moon. And no matter what happens as you grow up, no matter what choices you make, we'll always love you."

Cat felt herself getting misty as well.

"I love you too, Mom. And I'm fine, really."

Her mom sniffed, blinking back her tears before becoming her normal, practical self again.

"I know dear, but I wanted you to know how I felt. We haven't talked about the actual accident, and you haven't expressed much emotion about it. If you ever need to talk, you know your Dad and I are always here for you."

Cat reached over, patting her mom's hand.

"I know, Mom. But I don't have any emotions about the accident, honestly. I don't remember it at all. I just woke up after it was over. I think Vanessa is probably having a harder time. She hasn't said anything, but she got to see the whole thing, and she was driving. I think she feels guilty."

Cat stopped talking for a second, and thought about it.

"Actually, Mom, you may want to pry a bit with her. I haven't heard Vanessa say anything about the accident, and that's a problem. You know how dramatic she is, unless it's something important."

Her mom looked at her thoughtfully.

"You know, I think you may be right, Cat. She hasn't said a thing, other than the usual worry about you, and how school is hard. But she hasn't discussed the events of that night since it happened. Maybe try to get her to open up to you? She may be more willing to complain to you instead of her folks."

Cat shrugged.

"I'll try. But she may not want to talk to me either if she's feeling responsible."

Her mom nodded.

"We can both try. But for now, lets celebrate my baby feeling good again!"

Her mom smiled, and the conversation turned to happier things.

CAT SPENT THE REST of the week researching at home. She found a lot of vague information on what a firebird was, as well as a lot of stuff in other languages and about other countries. Each culture seemed to have a legend of a firebird, a phoenix, or some other type of magical bird, but they were all different. Traditional Greek mythology compared it to the sun, with a nimbus or aura around it. Sometimes it was a bird, or rooster, or even a peacock. Generally, it seemed to be a bird-like creature with sapphire eyes in European traditions. The Russians called it the firebird, with glowing fire-like plumage and eyes, and it was seen as both lucky and unlucky to those who captured it. Traditional Chinese versions represented power sent from the heavens to the Empress, and would only stay if the ruler was without darkness and corruption. In the Hindu tradition, it was the Garuda, the mortal enemy of the snake and any type of poison. And in every culture, it seemed able to heal and regenerate magically.

The main problem Cat had was that although every culture considered the creature's to be very powerful and magical, they were unclear on specific details. Accounts conflicted about what they could do and where they were found, and whether they were human or something else. Nothing Cat could find helped answer her questions, and it left her with more than she'd started with. She had so many things she'd love to ask Violet if she could see her again, not the least was why she'd told her she was a firebird in the first place.

She sadly thought about Violet again, and how she'd looked for her when she'd woken up. When Cat had asked the nurse about her, the woman had shook her head and said she'd passed away. She'd also missed her chance to talk to Violet's daughter, as she had been gone from the hospital for days. It felt like she'd let her down, and it still bothered her. Violet had opened her eyes to a new world and eased her transition, and it felt like a betrayal of her promise. Logically, Cat knew it wasn't her fault, but she still hoped the chance to fulfill her promise would return, someday.

Cat continued to research her brains out, but found it left her more confused. Deciding she needed a break, she went for a walk. It was lightly snowing, but she found herself warming up quickly from exertion. As she walked around the residential streets near the house, she found herself wondering if she could *make* herself see the lights, which she had now learned were auras. So far, she knew if she was happy she could see them, and also heal herself, although that could have been a fluke.

She tried to think herself warm, but didn't feel the tingle she associated with the other times. She then tried to think happy thoughts, feeling a little like Tinker Bell trying to help people fly, and giggled. This time, she felt a little flutter inside her chest. She looked around to see if there was anyone walking nearby. So far, she seemed to need proximity to others to see anything. She realized she'd reached the end of the street and decided to walk towards the downtown to see if she could work her new aura power around strangers. Feeling silly, she stared at people as she got into a more populated area, trying to balance staring with not being caught staring. Nothing was more awkward for someone who didn't like meeting new people than being caught staring. People may try to talk to her, ugh.

She saw a coffee shop ahead and decided to take a break with a hot cocoa, and watch while sipping. At least she wouldn't be as obvious with a prop. Everyone at a coffee shop people watched after all, it was expected. Cat ordered before picking a corner seat that allowed her to watch the staff, the room, and look at the passersby through the main window.

She thought of good moments from her past, and felt the glow start in her chest. The tingle spread down her arms and she felt alive in a way that she hadn't before, like she was bursting with health. As she looked around, people began to light up like Christmas trees, transforming from regular people to ones outlined in different shades of glowing beauty, as though a switch had been flipped.

The barista who had served her now had a spring-green, light coloured aura. The woman beside her stirring her coffee wearing a truly crazy hat had a darker purple glow, but without any of the mildewy dankness of Mr. Briggs in the hospital. Cat was awed by the different shades. Until now, she'd only seen light and dark, but looking around the room was like seeing the rainbow. Everyone had an overall impression of light to their auras, but in varying degrees and colours.

*Maybe it depends on the kind of person they are?*

For the first time in her life, Cat wanted to strike up random conversations with people. Her normal reticence won out, reluctantly, over her excitement.

*That would be crazy. I know I'd worry about someone's mental health if they randomly came up and started asking me questions.*

Instead, she continued to people watch until her drink was gone. She walked home deep in thought, but also more aware of people around her then she'd ever been before.

*School could be interesting on Monday. I hope I'm able to concentrate!*

AS SHE ARRIVED AT THE house, she met Vanessa walking home from school. Cat used her 'new eyes' to look at her sister, and frowned. Vanessa's aura appeared tarnished, and was a muted greyish-purple instead of silver like her mom's had been.

"How's it going?" Cat asked with concern.

Vanessa looked at her and shrugged.

"Oh, hey. School was pretty boring today. Some stupid assembly we had to sit through on drinking and driving."

Cat thought she saw her sister tense up when she said the word driving, and wanted to ask about it, but stopped when she saw Vanessa's expression. She couldn't remember ever seeing her look so down. Hoping to lighten the mood, she extended an invite.

"Hey, at least it's Friday, right? Any plans for the weekend?"

"Nope. Didn't feel like doing anything. I was invited out to the movies with some people, but I'm feeling a little too blah to go."

Vanessa shrugged again and put her coat and shoes away sluggishly.

"Want to see if Mom'll let us order some pizza? We could do our own movie night here, watch some old ones we liked when we were kids?"

Vanessa looked at her, head tilted, considering the offer.

"Yeah, sure. Why not? I don't want to stay up too late though, I'm pretty tired."

Cat smiled and crossed her heart.

"Promise. I'll go and ask if you want to pick out some movies? Meet you in the family room?"

Vanessa agreed, and Cat raced off.

Vanessa definitely wasn't herself. Cat hadn't spent much time with her since coming home from hospital. She'd generally gone to bed early with headaches, and Vanessa had been at school during the day. But today was Friday, and Cat was feeling more like herself. Her mission for the weekend was to get her sister back to her normal, slightly overdramatic, and out-going self.

She found her dad sitting in the den, going through paperwork on his desk.

"Hey Dad! Can we have pizza tonight? It's Friday, and I think we should have a family night."

He looked up absentmindedly.

"Hmmm? Sure, honey. Whatever you want. No anchovies."

He went back to the spreadsheets he was looking at without missing a beat. Cat knew that expression. She could probably buy twenty pizzas and he wouldn't notice. Well, until he got the Visa statement. He for sure noticed those.

It was unlikely he'd even be joining them for supper if he stayed in the den. Peter McLean was a hard worker, and often forgot to take care of basic needs like food and drink when he was wrapped up in a project. Cat was prone to that herself, which was the complete opposite of her mom and Vanessa, who often had difficulty finishing projects due to their artistic ideas causing them to start new projects before finishing old ones. Brushing away her scattered thoughts, Cat headed to the kitchen to look at her options. She eventually decided on Pizza Hut. No point in getting something greasy unless you went all out.

The pizza took forever to arrive. Now that Cat was awake, she had almost two weeks of not eating to make up for. She'd managed to put a few pounds back on, but still didn't like how prominent her collarbones were or how hollow her cheeks looked. She liked to have a bit more padding on her butt for sitting in the desks at school as well. Nothing like showing up with a cushion first day back, she snorted with amusement. After paying the delivery boy, she hollered for everyone to come eat. She grabbed herself a plate and a diet coke before sitting down in the family room. The first one to arrive was her mom, back from running errands and starving from the looks of her plate, with four pieces stacked high.

"Holy crap, Mom, seriously?"

Her mom smiled sheepishly.

"I skipped lunch today. And I'm feeling too lazy to get up and get seconds when I'm done my firsts."

As Cat expected, her dad didn't show up right away, but in the end he did come and sit with them.

"How's work going?" Cat asked over a bite of food.

"Pretty good," he said, after chewing the pizza in his mouth pointedly, causing Cat to flush at his silent correction of her talking with her mouth full.

"I figured I should take a break, and have a nice evening with my best girls. After all, it isn't every day we have a chance to do this, now that you guys are getting so old."

Her dad looked away at the end of the sentence, covering a suspicious sparkle in his eyes with another bite of pizza. Cat knew he was thinking about the accident, but in his typical, understated way he didn't come out and say anything.

Vanessa was the last to show up. She'd not only changed into fuzzy flannel pjs and slippers, but she'd brought a collection of movies to chose from.

"Here. Take a look through these and pick your favourite. I'm going to get some food."

Cat picked up the DVDs her sister had placed on the couch and looked through them. Some really old ones were there, such as *Escape to Witch Mountain, The Secret Garden, The Goonies*, and *Harry Potter*.

It was a no-brainer for Cat. At this time of year, with the weather getting colder, she always needed to enter the magical world of Harry Potter.

"You guys up for a *Harry Potter* movie marathon this weekend?"

Her mom and dad shrugged noncommittally, but her mother replied.

"Sure honey, but don't worry about us. Keep watching when we aren't here. I don't think we have time for all the movies in one weekend, but you girls go ahead."

Vanessa came back just as the decision was being made. She saw what Cat was holding and grinned ruefully.

"I should have known if I brought those they'd be your first choice."

Cat smiled back proudly.

"Let's spend the weekend with Harry, okay? He's a cute boy who'll never do us wrong!"

Vanessa rolled her eyes, but agreed.

"Hey, why not? I don't really want to do my homework anyways."

Her mom cleared her throat and frowned.

"Um, I mean, I can do my homework while watching, since I've seen them so many times I won't even be distracted."

Vanessa smiled innocently back at her mom, who shook her head with amusement. Cat looked at her family and felt the newly familiar warmth spread through her chest, taking the opportunity to look at each of them in turn.

Her mom's aura shone like the moon, while her dad had a more subdued, but still peacefully glowing, blue tinged one. Vanessa's was still darker then she thought it should be, but instead of the darkened silver Cat had seen when she'd arrived home, it was now more like an old pearl, and had lightened considerably, so she could see a shimmer of light. Maybe all it would take to make Vanessa shine was some sister time, helping her to get over the sadness of the accident. As Vanessa put the first movie into the machine, Cat snuggled into the couch to watch with a blanket and pillow. She planned to just enjoy spending time with her family, after all they'd been through in the previous month.

The rest of the weekend passed pleasantly in a similar fashion. Their parents had, true to their word, been in and out as they did whatever it was they needed to be doing. Their dad did some of his paperwork in the room while they watched through *The Philosopher's Stone, The Chamber of Secrets,* and *The Prisoner of Azkaban.* Cat found herself watching closely as they introduced Fawkes the phoenix, and wondered how accurate J. K. Rowling had been with her descriptions. It sounded like many of the legends Cat had come across, but she thought the healing tears were a stretch. And she definitely couldn't carry very much or sing a song that made people happy. She was lucky if they didn't tell her to shut up, she thought, a little sourly. She loved singing, but the world had so far said 'that's nice, don't do it right here, mmm k?'

Vanessa brightened a little more with each movie as the weekend drew closer to Monday. As Sunday evening came, they were only on the first half of the final movie. Their mom was happy they'd managed to finish their homework and even gone outside for a walk once a day. Vanessa was also happy because they'd escaped having to do any chores, even with their mom on a cleaning kick. Cat was simply happy she'd had the chance to hang out with her family.

They hadn't talked about much of importance though, since Cat had waited for Vanessa to bring up any concerns. She thought it was too early to push her sister yet, so she hadn't. At least Vanessa seemed to have a normal-looking aura by the end of *The Half Blood Prince,* which Cat counted as a win. They decided to finish the last two movies after school during the week, if school work allowed, and went to bed.

Cat felt equal parts of trepidation and excitement about the idea of finally getting back to her normal life. Monday was going to be interesting.

# CHAPTER SEVEN
# BACK TO SCHOOL

CAT OPENED THE CAR door and leaned over, giving her mom a hug.

"Have a good day, sweetie," said her mom, as she gave Cat a reassuring pat on the arm. "Try not to stress too much."

"Ha!" Cat laughed. "Now why would I stress? I've only missed the last three weeks after going to school for a week. What could I possibly have to worry about?"

Her mom smiled and patted her cheek.

"Try to have fun anyway."

She put the car in gear and drove away with a wave, as Cat took a deep breath and walked into the school.

It always felt a bit anti-climactic, when you'd been away for awhile and thought you'd get more attention on your return than you wanted. Then instead, you ended up not even being noticed, as Cat found the case to be upon entering the school. Cat wasn't upset. She'd thought she'd be stared at more, but was perfectly fine with only the occasional curious glance in her direction. She'd managed to finish, and thankfully understand, all the homework Vanessa had brought home, so she was able to keep up in her classes during the morning.

Lunch could be awkward, she thought as she entered the cafeteria. Vanessa had friends now, and Cat hadn't been at school for so long she wasn't sure if she was allowed to sit with her sister, or if she'd be left to sit alone. Cat had brought her own lunch, so skipped the line and looked around at the long tables for a place to sit. She saw a few people she vaguely recognized, but no one she felt comfortable going over to.

She'd just noticed an empty place near the back when she felt a tap on her shoulder.

"Hey girl. How've you been?"

She turned around and saw Evelyn standing with Denae, both holding lunch trays.

Cat shrugged.

"Hey. I'm okay. It was a bit of a wild ride. How are you?"

Evelyn smiled at her.

"How 'bout we go sit, and catch up?"

"Sure, I'll follow you guys."

Cat gestured for the girls to go ahead, following them to a nearby table. She sat with them, relieved that she wouldn't have to eat alone. Expecting that the girls would have a lot of questions, Cat waited. Instead, Evelyn began to fill in the blanks on what had been happening since Cat had been away.

"You've been gone a few weeks, so here's what you need to know. Obviously, you've missed a few tests, but nothing exciting. We're still doing *A Midsummer Night's Dream* in English, but our group has been short two people since you've been away so we've got an extension on the group work. Now you're back, we should be able to catch up."

Cat looked at her, confused.

"Who else was missing?"

Evelyn looked at her sadly. "You don't know? No one told you?"

Cat shook her head, brow wrinkled.

Denae shook her head sympathetically and filled her in.

"It was Robert, from our group, who was the other driver. In your car accident."

Cat looked at the girls, stunned and horrified.

"What? How?"

Cat shook her head in disbelief, trying to collect her thoughts.

"I don't remember anything from the accident. I hit my head, and spent two weeks in a coma in hospital. They just told me that the other driver had died, but I didn't know who it was. I never thought it would be anyone I knew!"

Cat put face down in her hands.

"Poor Robert. I didn't really know him but that makes it even worse."

Evelyn gently touched her arm.

"It isn't your fault. From what I've been able to get out of the grapevine, it sounds like Robert had just dropped Declan off after basketball practice and something happened, they aren't sure what, to make him drive erratically."

Denae nodded.

"He'd been seen by a few other drivers, running stop signs and red lights all the way to where he ran into you guys. It wasn't drugs or alcohol, they tested him for that, but even if they hadn't, Robert wasn't that kind of guy. They said it was almost like he'd had a stroke or heart attack, except he was too young, and they couldn't find any signs of it physically."

Evelyn's face was drawn and serious.

"I'll miss him. We go all the way back to grade six, when he used to bug me with spit balls."

It was Cat's turn to try to comfort her now.

"I'm sorry Evelyn. I wish we'd been a few seconds earlier or later."

Cat couldn't believe the other driver had been a classmate. She hadn't asked. She hadn't really wanted to know, but she'd just kind of assumed it was a drunk old man, not someone her age that she'd talked to the day of the accident. She replayed what she'd heard, and realized Evelyn had mentioned Declan.

*Robert had dropped Declan off, and then died afterward.*

She thought about what Dorothy had said at the hospital, about how she'd been fine until a boy had bumped into her. Then people thought she'd had a stroke and Dorothy said she couldn't get better because part of her soul was missing.

Was it possible the reason she didn't like Declan was because she'd sensed darkness on him, even before the accident? She remembered the dank underwater feeling she'd experienced whenever she was around Declan, realizing it was similar to how she'd felt in hospital when she'd touched the people with darkness in their auras. She was almost scared to see him again to have it proven true. She had no idea how to use her powers, and Cat had the sinking feeling there was more danger lurking here than she was prepared for.

*Oh Dorothy, we are so not in Kansas anymore.*

CAT PASSED THE REST of the day in a fog. English had been awkward, due to the setup of the classroom, and the now empty desk across from Cat. Even though she'd tried to ignore it, she could feel Robert's absence as though he was right there with them. It felt wrong, somehow, to talk about the play without him contributing an idea or two. Cat felt closer to Evelyn after their lunch period spent talking about the accident, but it was still uncomfortable sitting with the girls during spare, with the accident looming over Cat like a accusation, even if only in her own mind.

She came to the decision that if there was a threat out there that could take souls, she needed to determine the nature of her abilities and if possible, figure out how to protect herself and others from whatever the threat was. She pulled out her homework, ostensibly to start on it during study break, but instead looked off into the library, attempting to recreate how she'd last seen auras. As she'd noticed before, it was difficult when she wasn't happy. That was something that she'd need to work on. If there was an evil threat lurking, she'd need to be able to do her 'thing', whatever it was, at a moments notice. Most likely, it would be in a situation where she was scared or upset instead of happy.

At first she didn't see anything. She tried squinting, but couldn't see any better. She took a deep breath, and tried again, this time focusing on the feeling she remembered of warmth in her chest. Slowly, glowing lights began to appear around people. By concentrating on one person at a time, she saw different shades again, and this time noticed a pattern. People who she knew to be kind or happy seemed brighter, and those who looked sad had a duller sheen to their aura. A few of the more artistic and dramatic people she knew from Vanessa's crowd appeared to have purple tinges. Cat looked over at Evelyn and saw a strong red tinge with a white shimmer, almost like a fire opal. That must be because of her strong personality, thought Cat, smiling to herself. Denae's aura was a more muted, pleasant silvery-gold.

Cat continued to watch people, learning from what her eyes and heart told her. So far, she'd seen no sign of evil, but she began to notice small ripples around people. When she looked closer, she realized they all appeared to be injured or suffering from colds. She looked at the grouchy librarian who was always shushing everyone, and saw a disturbance in her aura around her head. When Cat looked with just her eyes, she saw that the librarian had taken off her glasses and was rubbing her eyes.

*Maybe she has a migraine.*

At that moment, Cat decided to see if she was able to do what she had done as a spirit and stood up.

She nonchalantly walked over to the desk.

"Excuse me, I was wondering if you had an extra copy of *A Midsummer Night's Dream*? I forgot mine at home."

Cat smiled at the librarian, hoping her ploy would work. The woman gave a frustrated sigh, possibly related to her headache or her personality, since as far as Cat was concerned the jury was still out on that one, and reached behind her.

"Here," she said. "Someone just dropped this copy off today. You can check it out."

Cat reached to grab the book, pretending to fumble. In the process, she let her hand rest on the librarian's, and tried to draw out the darkness she'd sensed in her aura.

She felt confusion in the woman, followed by a sense of relief, and an immediate improvement in the aura to a normal, nondescript, silver shade. Cat felt exhausted then just as quickly, she felt her energy begin to recover. She took the book with her and sat back down.

*Success.*

She was pleased with her achievement and hopeful that she was starting to understand what to do with her new-found abilities. But while she happy with the small success, she knew she hadn't begun to scratch the surface of what was possible. If only she could find someone to help guide her through this! It was too bad she didn't have a teacher for this class, she thought irritably.

As she walked out of school at the end of the day, Cat continued to observe the people around her. It was something she'd always been good at, considering that she liked to be around people but watch quietly instead of interacting.

This time, Evelyn noticed her and came over to her.

"Hey Cat, are you doing anything this week?"

Cat looked at her blankly, unsure where she was going with the question.

"Not really, no. Why?"

Evelyn shrugged.

"I was hoping you'd be able to get together and maybe study for the upcoming English test? I thought it'd be nice to do it together, and since you've been away for so long I can help if you had any questions."

"That would be great actually!" said Cat. "When were you thinking?"

"Well, the test isn't until next Tuesday, so maybe Saturday or Sunday? We can study on our own for the rest of the week, then go over things together closer to the test?"

"Sounds good to me! Did you want to get together at my house or yours? Or somewhere else, like a coffee shop?" Cat asked, open to anything.

"How about my house? Saturday around two? That way I can sleep in."

Evelyn grinned sheepishly, as she admitted her weakness.

"Yeah, that's right. I'm not a morning person."

"Totally agree!" said Cat, emphatically. "Mornings are always hard for me too, especially if studying is going to happen later."

Cat looked past Evelyn to see Vanessa standing with a group of people and noticed Declan was among the students around her. Cat must have had an odd expression on her face, because Evelyn looked at her intently.

"What is it?"

She followed Cat's gaze over to where Vanessa and the others stood, tilting her head slightly towards where Cat was looking.

"Is it Declan? There's something about him, isn't there?" Evelyn said, matter-of-factly, as if it were obvious. "Everyone always really likes him. He's a golden boy, really."

She said it without judgment, but Cat could tell she didn't like him, unlike everyone else.

"What do you mean?" Cat asked curiously, trying to draw Evelyn out so she could get to the bottom of her feeling about her, but the other girl just shrugged.

"He feels cold to me. I can't get a handle on it, but I don't like him. He's....different, somehow."

She laughed without humour, then changed subjects abruptly.

"Anyways, I have to go, my ride's here. See you tomorrow!"

With that cryptic comment, Evelyn disappeared into the mass of students leaving for the day.

Cat stood for a moment, watching the group of students around her sister. It appeared to be an impromptu meeting of people from the drama club. They all appeared to be relaxed, happy, and deeply engaged in conversation. Cat tried to read them, and was able to see a group of silvery-purple auras, with an occasional gold or blue one thrown in for good measure. It was only when she got to Declan that things got strange. It was the absence of light that fascinated her.

He didn't emit any glow, silvery or dark or coloured of any sort. It was as though he was a black hole, because as Cat watched she saw faint wisps of light going towards him from other people, disappearing in the area just above his skin. As she continued to watch, the people around him began to glow a little less bright, and dull patches developed around their auras. Just then, Declan looked at his watch, and must have said goodbye as everyone waved and he left. Most of the auras belonging to the others then began to lighten and return to normal, like a dimmer switch in reverse. Declan, however, didn't change.

Cat felt herself go cold, again feeling the sensation of being underwater. Was Declan was some sort of soul stealer? Like a psychic vampire? Cat wondered if that was even a thing. But what had she seen happening? If only she had someone she could ask about this stuff!

*Too bad there isn't some sort of Phoenix handbook that I could study.*

That she could handle. But before her accident, with the exception of a cameo in *Harry Potter*, She'd never heard of a firebird or phoenix.

"S'up."

Cat looked up at the sound of a voice and was startled to see Vanessa standing beside her. She hadn't seen her come over, she'd been so lost in thought. Cat used her new vision and didn't like what she saw in her sister's aura. She still had purple and silver, but she'd also developed patches of darkness that didn't look healthy. Much worse than they'd been on Friday before Cat had spent the weekend helping her relax. She gave her sister a big hug, one that appeared spontaneous to everyone, but Cat did it to see if she could fix the spots she'd seen.

*It worked!*

This time instead of a brief wave of fatigue like when she'd healed the librarian, Cat was overwhelmed by a feeling that hit her like a wall, and almost threw up. Vanessa had initially been surprised, but gave into the hug, relaxing against her sister and hugging her back.

She must have noticed when Cat had stopped because she stepped back and looked at her, frowning.

"What's wrong? You don't look very good."

Cat moved to a nearby bench and sat down, feeling drained and close to vomiting.

"Yeah, sorry. I guess my headache came back a little bit. Just suddenly feeling a bit sick."

Vanessa came and sat next to her.

"Are you sure you're ready to be back to school? I thought they wanted you to take more time off."

Cat shook her head.

"No really, I'm fine. This happens sometimes, no biggie. It doesn't usually last very long."

Even as she spoke, Cat could thankfully feel herself improving. When she saw Vanessa still looked concerned, she reassured her again.

"Really. I'm already better, I promise."

Vanessa didn't look convinced, but dropped it. Cat could see her aura looked healthy, and was a beautiful shimmery purple-tinged silver again. She breathed a sigh of relief, and saw their mom had pulled up, the last car in the lot, as always.

"Come on, Vanna White, Mom's here. Let's go. Hey, maybe we can convince her to get take-out again."

Vanessa smiled at Cat in amusement at the nickname, and together they went to meet their mom, with Cat pretending to be fine for her family's sake.

AS THE WEEK PASSED, Cat made a point to watch people with her aura-vison as they went by, and tried to heal when she could. It seemed to get easier with practice, and she found that her energy rebounded faster each time. At least, with little things. She also started to notice the area of a person's aura that showed a disruption or dull patch seemed to also be related to where the problem was. So, much as the librarian had had a headache, Cat could see where other people were suffering from illness. It was easy when people had something visibly wrong, like a cast or a sling. Cat was able to offer to help with opening a door or carrying a bag, and brush against them in the process. It worked best if she touched the person closer to the area indicating the issue. But sometimes it was difficult, like when she hadn't met the person before, or when it was a teacher.

Maybe it was possible to heal without touching, she thought. That would make it easier. Also, she grinned to herself, a little less creepy than being touchy-feely with a stranger.

She'd spent more time with Evelyn over the week, which was nice. She was different than the other students Cat had classes with. Although arguably Cat spoke as much with other members of her English group, she felt Evelyn might be someone that she could someday confide in, someone that could be more than just an acquaintance-friend.

Cat was also intrigued by Evelyn's aura. It was different than anyone else's, but not in scary way like Declan's. So far, most people had one main colour with a few sparks of another, or darkening in places that suggested something was wrong. But Evelyn had an beautiful aura that reminded Cat of an opal, with shimmers of white, silver, gold, and red. She wasn't sure what it meant, but she knew it felt good, and was pretty to look at.

By the time Saturday arrived, Cat was anxious to study. She wanted to have a chance to talk to Evelyn, away from other people. She needed to know why she'd said she didn't like Declan. From what Cat could tell, everyone else thought he walked on water, and what worried her most was how close Vanessa was to him. She couldn't help but feel that the fragile appearance of her sister's aura was somehow because of him. She only hoped Vanessa wasn't thinking about dating him, because it seemed like things could get bad fast if she did.

Cat had agreed to meet at Evelyn's place at two, and had left her house a few minutes beforehand. They'd discovered they only lived a few blocks apart, which was convenient as neither had a car. She'd brought her notes and copy of the book, but was hoping Evelyn's were better. Frankly, she'd missed two-thirds of class time spent on the book, so there was a solid chance that anyone's notes would have been an improvement.

She arrived at the address she'd been given the day before and rang the door bell. The house was a pleasant looking two story, with green and white trim. The door opened, but it wasn't Evelyn.

"Hello?"

Marie-Jean, the nurse Cat remembered from the hospital, stood in the doorway.

"Oh, um, hello," Cat stammered, nonplussed. She was momentarily confused, wondering if she had the wrong house, until Evelyn came to the door.

"It's okay, Mom, Cat's here to study, remember? I told you last week..."

Evelyn sounded exasperated as she trailed off, but Marie-Jean just smiled calmly.

"Yes, dear. I remember. Hello, Catherine, it's very nice to see you again. How've you been feeling? You look well."

Cat gazed at her, easily slipping into her aura-vision, and saw the same pattern she'd seen on Evelyn, only a little brighter, as though the colours were more mature.

Marie-Jean noticed the way Cat was watching her, and sharpened her gaze. "Hmmmm, I'm thinking you may be an interesting girl, very interesting."

Cat quickly switched her focus, but Evelyn's mother only smiled innocently. "Have a good time studying girls. I'll be in the kitchen, prepping food for the week."

She gave Evelyn a kiss on the cheek and waved at Cat, then was gone.

Evelyn rolled her eyes at Cat.

"Mothers. They're all the same. They want to cook for you and embarrass you. It's like a biathlon. I wonder if it's an Olympic sport?"

"It probably should be." Cat agreed, smirking at the thought of moms across the world coming together to compete.

"I figured we can study in the living room, since it has comfy couches and a big coffee table for our notes."

Cat nodded.

"Sounds good." She followed Evelyn on a brief house tour, with the highlights of bathroom and kitchen if she needed a drink. They quickly got down to work after setting up in the living room, working well with similar study styles.

After a few hours, Cat stretched stiff muscles and looked at her watch.

"Wow, look at the time!"

Evelyn looked at the clock on the wall and blinked with astonishment.

"Crazy! We've gotten a lot done today. We work well together."

She looked pleased with her announcement, until Cat laughed.

"What?" said Evelyn, frowning.

Cat shook her head dismissively.

"Nothing. Well, it's just, you sound so business-like when you say things sometimes. I totally see you as CEO of some multinational corporation in ten years."

Evelyn laughed, her frown dissolving.

"You and my mom both. In fact, I'm pretty sure my mom has my life already mapped out. I think because it's just the two of us, she watches me a little more closely than other parents would."

Her face softened with love.

"It's okay, though, my mom's had a hard life and she just wants mine to be better. I get that."

Cat looked inquisitively at her, cocking her head to one side while she waited for her to continue. Evelyn hesitated, eyes searching Cat's face before she seemed to decide something.

"My mom was born in Haiti, but immigrated when she was in her early twenties with my dad. They didn't have much but got by. My mom had taken nursing, so she could find work pretty much anywhere, and my dad did a lot of labour type jobs. He died in a work accident when I was just a baby."

Cat was about to say something, but Evelyn held up her hand to stop her.

"It's okay, I don't really remember him. But it was hard on my mom. Somehow, she managed to keep working and take care of me. She didn't know anyone, and didn't have any family to help. She was a feared by her community too, as some people thought she had 'the sight'. They were superstitious, and because of that thought it meant she was a Mambo, or a voodoo priestess."

Cat was engrossed, and leaned forward.

"Do you mean your mom can see...things? Like she has second sight?"

Evelyn thought for a minute.

"Yeah, I guess you'd call it that. She does seem to know things she shouldn't. And I sometimes feel things about people too, but not the same as she does."

Evelyn searched for the right words.

"I don't know how to explain it without sounding kind of like a crazy person, but sometimes I feel things about people. If I ignore them, more often than not I'll wish I'd listened to my gut, or intuition, or whatever you call it. Like you, Cat, you're different. There's something about you that's powerful but feels like it's still hidden. But since the accident, you feel like you're more awake."

Cat's heart leapt with excitement.

"Really? You can see that in me?"

Evelyn just shrugged. Cat wasn't quite ready to spill her details just yet, so changed the subject.

"What about Declan? What do you see in him that makes you not like him?"

Evelyn looked uncomfortable at the question.

"Declan feels wrong. Like there's some cold darkness in him. Haitians would call him a Bokor, which means a magician or sorcerer. He has power too, but I don't know what, just that it ain't good."

Cat could feel hope rising. Maybe there were some answers here for her. She felt she could trust Evelyn, but also wanted to talk to her mother. She still remembered when she had been a spirit in the hospital, and Marie-Jean had sensed her.

"What does your mom think? You know, about Declan?"

Evelyn thought for a moment.

"You know, I don't think she's ever met him. She doesn't come to school much and I don't think he's ever been sick since I've known him. He's only been here a bit over a year."

Cat knew her surprise must have showed.

"Astonishing, isn't it? said Evelyn. "The way everybody in town practically licks his feet, and he hasn't even been here very long."

"Yeah, actually, that isn't what I've typically experienced as the new kid. He's charming and all, but to have everyone that enthralled and to be in the middle of everything, well, that takes a lot of work."

Cat shook her head.

"I prefer to stay under the radar, but even Vanessa, who's super outgoing, doesn't have everyone in love with her the minute we move. That's actually the weirdest thing I've heard today."

Cat considered her next words carefully.

"Can I ask you something really important?"she asked, softly.

She waited for Evelyn to nod, and knew she had her complete attention.

"You know how I've been different since the accident?"

Evelyn nodded again, slowly.

"I am different, but I don't know how yet. Do you think your mom would be able to help me?"

At that, Evelyn jumped to her feet.

"Give me a minute, and I'll be back."

She looked at her watch.

"Maybe call your parents and ask if you can stay for supper. I think we'll want food if you're going to be here awhile."

Cat did as she suggested, calling her mom from the living room while Evelyn talked to hers. As expected, Mindy McLean was fine with Cat staying, but said she'd pick her up when she was done now that it was dark earlier in the evenings. Cat was to call her back when she was ready to go. Cat waited for what seemed like forever for Evelyn to come back, but in reality was probably only five minutes. When she returned, Marie-Jean was with her.

She smiled at Cat then walked around her, examining her from all sides before she stopped and sat down on the couch across from her.

"Oh, my dear, you're something aren't you?"

Cat shrugged.

"I don't know, actually. I was hoping you could help me figure out what that 'something' is. Evelyn says sometimes you know things."

Marie-Jean laughed, a big booming laugh full of humour.

"That's true. Sometimes for good and sometimes I'd rather not know, but there it is anyway. Now, child, what do you know about yourself? You're different than I remember. You shine brighter now."

Cat squirmed in her seat, but figured starting at the beginning would be as good a place as any.

"It was the accident, I think. When I was in the hospital I was... sleeping."

She paused, trying to pick her words so she didn't sound completely crazy.

"I talked to people, and saw people differently when I was unconscious."

Marie-Jean nodded.

"And what did you talk about?"

Cat squirmed again, feeling embarrassed at the faint blush she could feel beginning to creep up her neck.

"Well, it was all very strange. I woke up in the hospital and talked with a woman named Violet first, who said she'd had a stroke. She wanted me to tell her daughter, Carol, it was okay, that she loved her and was ready to die."

Cat felt sad thinking about Violet, and looked at Marie-Jean with regret.

"I never got a chance to tell her. She was gone when I woke up."

Marie-Jean and Evelyn waited, looking at her to continue.

"I also saw two people on the other side of a door. It was in the hospital and these people were alive, but they had heavy darkness around them. One was named Mr. Briggs and the other was an old woman named Dorothy. I did something to them when I touched them. It felt like I healed them."

Cat stopped talking, feeling totally crazy.

"So that explains it."

Marie-Jean looked pleased, as though she'd known something and just had her suspicions confirmed.

"Explains what?" Cat asked, confused again.

Marie Jean smiled at her.

"I knew there was something different going on while you were there, but I couldn't figure it out. Those people you met in your dream, they were real people, cher."

Cat looked relieved.

"So does that mean I'm not crazy?"

Marie-Jean laughed.

"Well I don't know nothing about that, but the people you were seeing really exist. That Dorothy walked right out of the hospital before you woke up, completely back to her normal self. She was pretty pleased to go. And Mr. Briggs? Why, he looked the most peaceful I'd ever seen him. He's still very sick, but looked happy when he went home. Like he was ready to go, come what may, and had lost the deep bitterness he'd had when he came in."

Cat took a deep breath, relieved.

"So it wasn't just a dream then. It really happened."

"But what happened, Cat?" asked Evelyn. "How did you heal them?"

Cat turned back to Marie-Jean.

"Violet said I was something called a firebird. I've tried to find out what it means, but so many different versions exist, depending on the culture, and all of the explanations are really vague."

Marie-Jean looked thoughtful again, but didn't speak.

Cat shrugged.

"From what I've been able to figure out, it seems I can regenerate and heal. I'm not really sure how to do either though, I've just been muddling along."

Evelyn clapped her hands delightedly.

"That's awesome! Just think of all the things you can do! Is that why you've been so intense at school lately? With all the staring and bumping into other people?"

Cat blushed even harder.

"I was kind of hoping it wasn't obvious. I've been trying to figure out how to use this power, I guess you could say. I still have no idea why or how I've got it, and have no one to show me how to use it."

Marie-Jean got up and slowly walked around the room, quiet and thoughtful. Both Cat and Evelyn watched her without speaking, waiting for her to do something. Finally, after the suspense was almost killing them, she spoke.

"My village talked about a great spirit of good, sent to the people during times of great evil to deliver them. This spirit was made of fire, and came from the sun on the wings of a bird with the eyes of the sky. It was said it could heal with a glance, and restore people's spirits when they'd been taken by this great evil, and nothing could injure it or keep it caged. This bird of fire was immortal and untouchable, eternally pure."

She looked at Cat appraisingly.

"You certainly have eyes of the sky and hair of the sun. But you say you've never heard of this creature before your accident? There aren't any family stories or legends?"

Cat looked at her and Evelyn before glancing away, ducking her chin.

"I haven't talked to my family about this yet. I didn't know what to say, and after the accident and how awful it was for everyone, I couldn't add this extra stress for them to deal with. But to answer the question, no, I've never heard any legends or anything like this until now."

Marie-Jean nodded again.

"If you can, ask. Maybe your mother or father have heard stories from their parents. You may find out more than you expect by looking into your family tree."

She sniffed the air.

"Come. Supper's ready, and we can discuss more over food."

BY THE TIME DINNER was over and the evening had come and gone, Cat was left with more questions than answers. Yet for the first time, she also felt as if she might have people she could count on to help her. Given the way she felt about Declan, that was probably going to be a good thing. It was like Violet had warned, a great darkness was coming, and she knew it would be up to her to bring back the light.

If she could only figure out what that meant.

# CHAPTER EIGHT
# FAMILY TREE

CAT SPENT THE REMAINDER of the weekend going for walks in between spurts of studying. The session at Evelyn's had been useful for her test, but it was the other discussion that kept repeating in her head. She hadn't had a chance to talk with her parents yet, and was still trying to figure out how she could bring up the topic without sounding as though she had brain damage from the accident. When she came back into the house, she went to the den first. Maybe she could ask her dad. He enjoyed reading, and often knew about weird or rare things.

*May as well start with an expert.*

She entered the room to find him sitting at his desk, on his computer. He'd been spending most of his free time since they'd moved trying to become an expert on his current branch, as well as keeping up with the stock market. He looked up when her heard her enter, then smiled before rubbing his eyes, stretching his arms out at the same time.

"Hey, honey, how are you?"

She leaned over and gave him a hug.

"Good, Dad. How long have you been doing that? You look wiped."

Her dad gave her a rueful smile.

"Thanks. It's always good to know when you look like crap."

Cat punched him lightly on the arm.

"Daaaaad!" she whined, with a twinkle in her eyes.

He smiled and leaned back.

"Did you want something? You look like you have a question."

Cat took a deep breath, and plunged in.

"Dad, do you know anything about a firebird?"

Her dad looked confused.

"You mean the car? I've always wanted one."

"No dad, like an actual bird, like, out of mythology."

He leaned forward in his chair, looking at her curiously.

"Why do you ask?"

*Crap. I knew he was going to ask me that.*

"Dad, something really weird happened while I was in the hospital. I saw a woman in my sleep. She told me I was a firebird, and the there's a darkness coming. But I don't know what that means. I was kind of hoping maybe you could help with some answers?"

Her dad sighed deeply, as though he'd been expecting her to ask this question, but had been dreading it.

"What are you worried about?" her dad asked, waiting for her to continue.

Cat shook her head impatiently.

"I don't even know what to be worried about! Nothing's been the same since the hospital, and I need to know if this has happened before. " she said, wrinkling her brow. "I was hoping that there was something you've heard or read about that could help."

"Yes, actually, I've heard stories. Way back, in Scotland, there was talk about one of our ancestors being a firebird. The details are vague, but the legend says they were of the Sidhe and very powerful, and were friends with Robin Goodfellow as well. How it started isn't clear, but the first stories come from around the time of the Battle of Bannockburn in 1314, when the Scottish were fighting against the rule of Edward II of England. They say the reason the Scottish were able to turn the English forces during the battle was due to the efforts of a man, who, 'Shone bright as the sun, who not only fought with great skill but seemed to be impossible to kill,' to quote the records."

Cat had found a chair, and sat as her dad took her into the past with his storytelling.

"Who were the Sidhe?" she asked curiously.

"They were what some call fairies, or elves. Magical creatures that were different and powerful and often feared."

He stopped briefly to answer her question before he continued.

"The Scottish only lost only 500 men in that fight, with many men who'd had seemingly serious wounds instead turn out to be scratches, while the English lost ten thousand men more, even though they'd had at least three times the number of men at the start."

Cat looked at her dad, remembering what he'd said at the beginning.

"Wait a minute- do you mean the same Robin Goodfellow from Shakespeare?"

Her dad nodded.

"Many people say Shakespeare got his ideas from the legends of people from the time. Robin Goodfellow was highly thought of by superstitious people. He was either a fairy or an elf, or possibly had been an old god of the land, once worshipped but fallen out of power ages ago. Those in his favour were known to prosper and have bountiful crops. But woe to those who angered him! They were as likely to have crops fail or mice infest their homes, or disappear with the Wild Ride if it went by."

He smiled mischievously and wiggled his eyebrows.

"The wild ride were supposed to be the souls of the damned chasing sinners to add to their gang. At least, that's one version."

Cat looked at him with wonder.

"How do you know any of this?"

He looked at her uncomfortably, took a breath then looked into the distance.

"Our family history goes back a long, long way. It's always been the job of the oldest child to keep the history, long before our ancestors moved to North America during the Highland Clearances of the 1800's. The McLeans are one of the oldest families in the Highlands, and have been associated with otherworldly events for centuries. Having 'second sight' is very common and quite respected in the Highlands."

Cat took another look at her dad, this time with her other vision. She noticed more than just the blueish shimmer, catching glimpses of green and yellow shifting within, almost as though he was a clear lake.

"Do you have any 'otherworldly' abilities, Dad? Do you know anyone in the family that does? When do you find out? Are people born with it?"

Her dad laughed at her machine gun-like barrage of questions.

"Woah there, honey! I'll try to answer your questions, if I can remember all of them."

Cat smiled, sheepishly.

"Sorry, Dad."

He waved away her chagrined apology.

"No problem. Okay, first question. I don't have any great abilities, although I do have a small affinity for water and can sometimes see images, or get feelings about things if I'm near it. There's a legend of Selkie blood in the lineage, but almost every family from the Highlands says that, so who knows if it's true."

Cat looked at him, confused.

"What's a Selkie?"

Peter stopped again and smiled.

"Yes, I guess you wouldn't know that word. A Selkie is a creature who lives in the sea as a seal, but can shed their skin to become human on land. They will often mate and marry with a human, then leave to return to the sea, often never seeing their family again."

He stopped and rubbed his face again, although he looked much less tired than when she'd first entered the room.

"Now, for your other questions. Some people don't find out about their abilities until their teens. My mother was like that. She was sixteen when she developed the sight. She was a powerful seer, though she spoke rarely about it."

He looked at Cat seriously, more seriously then she could remember seeing him, unless she'd done something really, really bad, which made her nervous. He sighed deeply and spoke again, as though telling her a dark secret he already regretted sharing.

"She saw you. Before you were born, she prophesied you would be born with hair of fire and eyes of sky."

Cat looked at him, every inch of her screaming for more information.

He leaned over and brushed her hair off her face, looking at her intently.

"She said you'd be special and powerful, and one like no other. Like no one had seen in generations. And she said that you'd be needed to fight a darkness that would try to cover the land. She left this for you, for the day when you would come to me, needing answers."

He dropped his hand, reaching over to his bookshelf beside the desk, grabbing a small book and handing it to her.

Cat examined it closely, realizing it looked like a journal. She looked at her dad. "What is it?"

He opened the front page for her.

"This is the book your grandma wanted me to give you. She knew she wouldn't be here when you came into your gift, but she wanted to help you learn to control it. She wanted you to have this when you started to ask questions."

Cat held the book to her chest.

"Thank you, Dad."

She brushed her hair back again.

"Mostly, thanks for not thinking I'm crazy. I was really worried you would."

Her dad just smiled at her.

"Not me, honey. Your mom may not understand, but I think you may have some help from Vanessa, if you talk to her about this."

Cat shook her head.

"I'm not sure she's ready for anything weird. She's just starting to look better from the accident,"she said, then shyly added, "her aura was all dark and tarnished for awhile. It's looking better now, but I'm still worried about her."

Her dad agreed.

"Vanessa will be a great ally for you, but she may need some time. Tell me, Cat, what can you do right now? You say you can see auras?"

Cat quickly ran through the basics with her dad, explaining how she could see auras if she was in the right mindset, and sometimes heal people by touch, and was starting to know what a person was like by the colour of their aura. Her dad was interested, asking her all kinds of questions about what had happened in the hospital and afterward. He was particularly interested in both the woman Cat had healed from her 'stroke' and Declan. She also told him about the boy who'd died, and her suspicion that it all connected back to Declan.

By the time Cat had finished retelling her dad everything, it was supper time. Her mother had yelled to them to come to the table, and they'd been startled, not realizing it was so late.

"I want you to take the book to your room and read it. Keep it in a safe place and please, come ask me if you need any help."

He smiled crookedly.

"Sometimes your grandma could be very oblique in her speech, and her writing could be even more confusing."

Cat agreed reluctantly, eager to read it but running upstairs to put the book away, mostly to keep her mom happy.

Supper was the usual affair with small talk around the table. Her mom was excited about an art gallery in the downtown that was expressing interest in displaying her paintings. Cat watched her talk, delighted to see her aura shooting sparks of silver and gold. She looked so happy. And her dad glowed while watching her mom as well, this time with love and pride enriching his blue and green. Vanessa was quiet, but her aura appeared a normal silvery-purple, and looked whole. Cat was still worried about her, but saw nothing to cause imminent panic about her sister's safety.

She didn't like Vanessa talking to Declan all the time, and knew it was likely sapping her energy, but at least her aura wasn't dark like it had been earlier in the week. She needed to figure out how to get Vanessa to believe her, and not think she was just wanting her to avoid Declan because of jealousy or something.

*After all, he's like the King of the school, and nice to everyone but wants to hang out with her. She'll totally think it's a sister-spite or jealousy thing unless I can convince her otherwise.*

ONCE SUPPER WAS OVER, Cat made an excuse about needing to study and went upstairs. She did briefly look at her notes for the test, so it wasn't exactly a lie. But she'd really wanted a chance to sit down and read the book her dad had given her. It was so cool to find out she wasn't the only freak in the family. From the sounds of it, she came from a long line of people who were different. Her dad had mentioned relatives from both sides of his family.

Apparently, it was common for Highland families to intermarry between different branches and into different families, concentrating the abilities further.

After learning the little that she had from her dad, it also made sense to her for the first time why her Scottish ancestors had been so superstitious. It was because they lived with it, and in it, and around it. Cat was eager to learn more, and turned the pages of the book, finding a letter tucked away at the beginning.

She opened it and read.

MY DEAR DARLING. I imagine your father has convinced your mother to name you Catherine, based on his love of history and the great Catherines of old. It is a good name, and it will serve you well. Much like Catherine the Great, you will do amazing things. I see what you will become and I am in awe. But you must be wondering how and why, and all of the thoughts that would go through your head at the dawning of your powers. I, too, remember the first flutterings and confusion that followed when I began to see and hear things that weren't there to others around me. I was lucky though, since my grandmother was there to help me. I wish I could be there to guide you, but I hope my words will be enough, as they are all I can offer. Your dad is wise in so many ways, but while he can touch the veil of the otherworld, he can not step through and experience its full majesty. He will never meet those of the Sidhe, and Robin Goodfellow is only a name to him. They are real and he believes, but because he can not see he is limited to scrying in water when events are already underway, or getting glimpses in standing water when the veil is thin.

Your sister will be a believer too, but her gifts are different, and will be sleeping for a time yet. If I am correct, you have already talked to the other side, and learned to read the spirit colours somewhat. This will get easier for you in time. You can also heal after a fashion, but nothing like what you will be able to do. You will be a glorious firebird, a gift from the heavens, and will burn off the evil that comes for others with the power of your soul. You will also be able to regenerate, but much as with the running you are born to do, and enjoy so much, you must practice, practice, practice.

This will help you to become strong and will make you grow wise. You must learn to unite the soul with the body and heal the broken. Only then will you be able to break the curse and free the vessel. This will be but the first step to fighting the great darkness, but you must do so in order to win the first battle. Sadly, my love, there will be many battles ahead for you. The world is large and in much need of healing. You will not be owned, but must be free to give your blessings where needed. Look to the stories of old, of the Sidhe, of Danu and Eire, and to stories of the spirits of the lands. Each culture has its superstitions. Look to the heart of them, and see the soul. You will find the truth with courage and by using your heart-sight. I will give examples in this book and tell you more of my visions, but you still must learn to do much on your own, so that you learn how it feels to do it. You will succeed, if you believe in the power of your soul and your friends. Yes, my dear, you will have helpers along this path. Trust in them, and help each other.

With all my love,
Fiona McLean

CAT FINISHED THE LETTER at the beginning of the book and sat staring out the window. It was fully dark now, but she could see the street lights and the street below. She had a lot to think about. It sounded as if she'd be able to heal without touching, and be able to read people better, and burn off evil while being untouchable herself. Was evil the darkness? She had to admit, it sounded pretty good. What was this part about Vanessa? She had powers too?

*I wonder what they are? And who was the vessel? Was she talking about Declan? Vessel for what or for who?*

Although she'd learned something from the letter, it had left her with more questions.

Cat flipped through the book, noting there was a great deal more writing, mostly short entries. She looked at her watch and sighed. Enough for tonight. Tomorrow would be soon enough to read the rest.

# CHAPTER NINE
# SISTERS UNITE

THE NEXT DAY CAT FELT like she was merely going through the motions with everything. It felt like Christmas, or like there was some big juicy surprise she was waiting to have happen to her. She felt like she needed to work on her new abilities and had a sense of urgency now she had an idea of what was ahead of her. The physical act of being in school was more painful than usual, although strangely, she felt she'd done well on her exam. *A Midsummer Night's Dream* was more relatable now. For the first time she believed the book was more history than fantasy, possibly even based on true events. A thought struck her out of nowhere. Maybe she should study the book afterwards, but this time to learn more about legends from an earlier time.

Somehow, she made it through the day. She met up with Evelyn after the exam for study period, and desperately wanted to talk to her about everything, but the grouchy librarian watched them like a hawk the entire time. They'd had to settle for surreptitiously passing notes, but it was difficult to get into any detail that way. Cat wished they had smart phones like everyone else, but her parents said she could have one when she could afford one or got her drivers licence, and Evelyn's mom just flatly refused to get her one. At least she wasn't the only one, Cat sighed to herself.

Cat had managed to tell Evelyn about the book and she'd been excited to see it. She also mentioned that she had to beat the 'vessel', and put a question mark and arrow to Declan's name, scratching it out after Evelyn had read it, in case anyone found the paper later. It was time to start figuring out what the situation was concerning him. Cat needed to start by getting background information, but wasn't sure how to do it. She wanted to bring Vanessa on board with what was happening as well, but hesitated. She was in the same class and hanging out with De-clan, but it was more because Vanessa was her best friend. Cat worried her mercurial sister would be mad at her on many levels. Firstly because she'd kept her in the dark, secondly because she was thinking bad things about Declan, and then whatever else she felt like being mad at because of the situation.

Cat sent another note to Evelyn.

'What should I do about finding out about the vessel? any ideas? should I ask my sister?'

Evelyn read the note and thought about it for a minute, before scribbling on the bottom and sending it back.

'Ask Vanessa. I'll check at the town library tomorrow after school and look at the news, police, real estate, anything I can get my hands on. Can we meet Wednesday after school? Drama starts then, we can pretend we're going and meet up instead.'

Cat read the note and nodded, replying at the bottom.

'Yes, but we have to actually go for a bit, Vanessa will want to be there. I have to figure out how to tell her. Maybe I can do it before, and she can cover for me. Or maybe we should go keep an eye on things? Let's talk tonight after school and figure it out.

Evelyn nodded, looking up to find the librarian watching her in-tently. She turned back to her open text book and focused pointedly on her work. Cat noticed, then reluctantly did the same.

Luckily, gym class at the end of the day meant the rest of the school day went fast. Cat promised to call Evelyn after finishing supper, as they had to keep talk to a minimum to avoid being overheard in classes. Both girls were having a hard time, as school couldn't compare to their new situation for excitement. They were sixteen, so being patient wasn't easy, although Cat wasn't sure she'd get any better at tolerating waiting with age.

After school, Cat met up with Vanessa, who this time wasn't with a group of people. Cat found her sitting on the steps alone, looking dejectedly into the parking lot. She gave a half-hearted wave when she saw Cat walking towards her.

"What's wrong, Vanessa? You look kind of... bummed," Cat said, worriedly examining her aura, which was still purple-silver, but now had a tarnished look again.

Vanessa shrugged.

"I don't know, just tired lately."

"Anything you want to talk about? I feel like I never see you anymore. How's everything going?"

Cat hesitated for a minute, and looked around.

"I miss you," she quietly added.

Vanessa punched her in the shoulder, her lip curling slightly.

"You're such a dork, Cat."

Cat noticed she looked a little happier, either from the brief contact or just at calling her names. Cat concentrated, and felt the warmth rise in her chest. As she watched, she could see Vanessa's aura brighten, like the sun reappearing from behind clouds. She wasn't a hundred percent sure, but it felt like she'd maybe healed her without touch this time.

Vanessa turned to her with an intense look.

"Do you ever feel like everything is just wonderful, but at the same time, you feel kind of empty and disjointed? That's how I feel these days. It's like, okay, home is good, I can tolerate my parents and sister, and I'm making new friends. And I really like them too. I'm super excited for drama club to start, but then at the exact same time, I feel hanging with people here is so exhausting that I can't wait to get home and chill and not see anyone."

Cat nodded sympathetically.

"I think I know what you mean. This may sound crazy, but I think it's just since we moved here I've felt like that. More since the accident, particularly."

Vanessa nodded emphatically, pointing her index finger at Cat.

"It's like everyone is so nice they drain the life out of you, right?"

Cat hesitated, then spoke again.

"What if I told you it wasn't everyone, but maybe that's what's really happening? Would you think I was crazy?"

Vanessa laughed.

"I always think you're crazy, Kitty-Cat. What could change that?"

Cat smiled with relief. Vanessa was acting like her normal self again, and maybe she'd be open to believing something freaky was happening.

"Can I talk to you at home about some stuff? Just the two of us?"

Vanessa looked intrigued, completely out of her funk now.

"How about we see if Mom and Dad are okay with us going out for coffee or something? We could go for a walk."

"Yeah, that sounds good. I really need to tell you some stuff, and its hard to talk about with people around."

Cat stumbled a little over her words, causing Vanessa to look at her with concern.

"Are you okay?"

Cat shrugged.

"I'm fine, it's nothing like that. I've been having some weird things happen lately, and I think I need some help to figure it out."

"Sure," Vanessa said, when, as usual, their mom pulled in just as the parking lot was emptying out.

TRUE TO HER WORD, VANESSA asked their parents if it was okay if they went for a walk and coffee after supper. Their dad mumbled something incomprehensible as he walked into the office with his head down that sounded like a general agreement, but their mom more clearly gave permission, providing they did the dishes. Quickly they tidied up, then dressed warmly and left the house. It was a good night for a walk, clear and crisp but not freezing.

Vanessa opened up conversation, surprising Cat.

"So you mentioned something about this town sucking the life out of you? When did you start to notice this?"

Cat took a moment to reply, not sure how to bring up Declan.

"Well, you know how I've always had feelings about people and stuff?"

She quickly glanced at her sister as they walked, catching her nod in response.

"Well, something about that accident seemed to jog something loose, or maybe strengthened something. During the time I spent in the hospital unconscious to you guys, I was actually awake, but out of my body. I discovered I could read auras, and it sounds silly, but I can heal people by touching them."

Vanessa stared at her, eyebrows raised.

"What? Are you serious?"

Cat raised one shoulder dismissively.

"Yeah, I know it sounds nuts. But Vanessa, I see the world so differently now. It's scary and amazing all at once. I healed a woman who had a stroke. And I don't know if you'll believe it or not, but I've also been healing you for the last few weeks."

Vanessa stopped in the middle of the street, the overhead streetlight casting dancing shadows around her with the wind as the trees moved behind her. Slowly, she relaxed as what Cat had said sank in.

"I wondered what was happening. I said I'd been tired, but it felt like more than just fatigue. It felt like I was losing a piece of my soul. Like my sense of self was somehow breaking, and I couldn't stop it. Even the stuff I enjoyed wasn't fulfilling anymore. But then after being around you I would feel lighter again, more like myself. How did you do it?"

Cat filled her in on what she had learned to do over the pervious few weeks, before coming to the hard part, watching Vanessa carefully as she spoke.

"I think Declan is the one causing all the strangeness lately. I think he's the one taking energy from people, and I think he's the reason Robert ran into us that night. Have you noticed everyone is always around him, but when they leave they're all tired? I think he's the reason you've felt so bad lately."

Vanessa shook her head.

"It can't be. Not Declan. He's too nice to do anything like that. Even if it was possible. How could it be him? He's just a kid, like us."

Cat disagreed.

"I don't think he is. I get the feeling he's been around a long, long time. But I need to find out more, because I think he's going to do something really big and really awful, but I don't know what."

Cat looked into her still skeptical face.

"I need your help," Cat implored.

"I just can't believe it's because of Declan. How? It's not humanly possible."

Cat exhaled impatiently.

"I don't know how. But do you believe me about what I'm seeing? I swear, I'm not making it up."

"I know you aren't." Vanessa said, "and yeah, I know you've always been different, so I'm not really surprised you are seeing weird shit now. But I'm not sure how to find out what you need to prove whatever it is you need to prove."

Vanessa pointed into the coffee shop at which they'd arrived.

"Let's go sit down. You can tell me more inside. I need something warm and I think I need to sit down."

The girls ordered hot chocolate and found a comfortable set of over-stuffed chairs in front of the fireplace.

"Who else knows about this?" asked Vanessa, as she blew on her drink before taking a delicate sip, watching Cat intently.

"Just Dad, and my friend Evelyn and her mother."

Vanessa looked surprised, temporarily forgetting her drink.

"Dad, I understand, but your friend's mom?"

"She was my nurse in the hospital and she can see things." Cat explained.

"Of course she can," said Vanessa, appearing resigned to accepting everything Cat was telling her now.

"What about Evelyn?"

"She's never liked Declan. She's got a little bit of her mother's power, but she's not as strong yet. Basically, she got the willies from him right from the start and never got close to him the way everyone else has. She's going to go look at the library tomorrow to see what she can find out about his background. Is there anything you know about him? You guys have been hanging out a lot."

Vanessa thought about it for a moment, and for the first time since they'd started talking, looked truly surprised.

"You know what, I actually don't know anything about him. I don't know where he lives, and I don't think I've ever heard him talk about his family. He always turns the conversation to someone else, now that I think about it. I think that's part of why everyone likes him so much."

She took another sip of her drink.

"That's really weird. I spend half my classes with him, and I'm in drama club on Wednesdays, and I don't know much more than his name."

Cat agreed it was odd.

"So you believe me then? Will you help?"

Vanessa nodded.

"Of course I'll help you. We're sisters. You may be a lot of things, but you've never lied to me."

She gave her a wry look, as she lifted her hands in surrender.

"This is just one more of the weird things I'll try to trust you on. I may not believe Declan is doing anything, but I'm willing to see what we can find out. After all, I'm stuck with you in life, I may as well own it."

# CHAPTER TEN
# RESEARCH MODE

OVER THE NEXT FEW DAYS, Cat, Vanessa, and Evelyn decided that they'd go to the drama club meeting together, in order to get closer to Declan in a safer group setting. Afterward, they would meet up to discuss their findings. Evelyn would go to the library to see what she could find online or in print, and Vanessa would try to learn something about him the old-fashioned way, by asking him questions about himself, and spending as much time with him as she could. It wouldn't seem weird, as they already shared a lot of classes, and until her conversation with Cat, Vanessa had been seeking him out for company most days.

Vanessa was embarrassed that she hadn't done this earlier. It wasn't normal for her not to be curious about other people. Usually, she was the one trying to get strangers to open up about themselves, and part of why she had no problems fitting in when they moved was because she was really good at it. It was almost as though Declan had deflected any interest in himself by being interested in others. Or, as Cat believed, by taking away some of their soul so they didn't have enough energy left to ask him any inconvenient questions.

Cat planned to keep practicing her new abilities to read auras and heal people, and would to try to see what else she could find out in her grandma's journal. In between classes, homework, and keeping both sets of parents happy, of course. It helped that both Evelyn's mom and Cat's dad were aware otherworldly things were brewing, but it also made things a little awkward, trying to figure out how much to tell them to keep them informed without worrying them.

Wednesday came quickly, and Vanessa did her best to talk to Declan before the drama club meeting. She caught him outside English, just as Mr. Grayson shut the door behind the departing students.

"Hey, Declan! Wait up!"

Vanessa swung her long dark hair behind her back casually, as she pretended to fumble her backpack.

Declan, always the gentleman, helped her by deftly catching a strap and taking the weight off her arm.

"Hey, Vanessa. Wow, this is heavy! What all do you have in this thing?"

Declan raised a perfect eyebrow and gave her a curious half smile.

Vanessa giggled, unable to stop the sound from slipping out.

" Oh, thanks! Yeah, I know it's crazy. I have some text books in it today. I thought I'd try to get a head start on a couple of assignments. Hey, are you going to Drama tonight?"

She batted her eyelashes at him in a subtle way and noticed his apparent interest with satisfaction.

"Yeah, I was planning on it. I'm going to run home first, grab a bite, but then I'll come back. Starting to get pumped about this years play. I think it'll be tight. You?"

Vanessa dipped her head.

"I wouldn't miss it. I was kind of hoping I'd run into you before, see what you've been doing. I feel like it's been forever since we had a chance to sit and talk."

She looked up through her eyelashes, trying to gauge his expression. She could tell that he was interested in her not-so-subtle attempt at flirtation, but was struck now by his eyes. She'd never noticed before speaking with Cat that his eyes were a hard, dark brown, so dark they appeared black. As she watched, his face was as attractive as always, but now she only felt coldness instead of the warmth she remembered from before.

"I've missed seeing you around too. Do you want to maybe get a drink after, or something?"

He gave her a suave smile, and she felt as if her heart had jumped up into her throat.

"Oh, jeez, I'd totally love to, but I have to take my sister home. Maybe soon. Can I catch you at lunch tomorrow maybe?"

As much as Vanessa wanted to ask him questions, she couldn't help but feel being alone with him was a bad idea. Already she felt tired and knew it was due to her proximity to him in the hallway.

"Hey, do you have any brothers or sisters? They're such a pain, hey?"

Declan shook his head.

"No, it's just me. Only child, here. I guess you could say I'm a little spoiled."

A strange smile curled his lips, but his eyes stayed cold, and Vanessa shivered. He was so beautiful. It wasn't fair.

"Well, do you have any plans for the rest of the term?" Vanessa probed, trying to get something, anything, from him before she left.

Declan ran his fingers through his perfect dark blond hair and scratched his chin.

"Nah, man. I'm just hanging out. I'm pretty busy between sports and drama club." Vanessa nodded, then made a show of looking at her watch.

"Oh, God! Look at the time! I'm sooooo sorry, Declan. I'd love to stay and chat but I have to run! I'll see you tonight, okay?"

She took back her bag, giving him a light peck on the cheek, then wiggled her fingers in a wave. She took a quick look over her shoulder to see him standing there, watching her with the same dark, impenetrable half smile.

That made her even more determined to get something on him, anything, even if it was just what his favourite colour was. If there was one thing she was above all else, it was determined. Vanessa could usually get information out of a stone, but trying to get details from Declan was like talking to Teflon.

She decided to ask around, pretending she was interested in him and playing the teen crush angle. Usually that worked, as she found people were more likely to talk if they thought they were sharing juicy secrets. Yet the only information Vanessa got was pitiful. Over the year or so since Declan had moved to town, he hadn't had a girlfriend, or boyfriend, and had no one people could identify as a best friend. He was in almost every group, teachers liked him, he did well in classes and sports, and consensus was that he most likely would be crowned King Of The World by the end of the school year. But when she asked directly, people seemed as confused as she'd been at the fact they didn't know more, as though they had thought they did, but the information was missing when they looked for it.

Vanessa couldn't help but think that this was proving her sister right. How could someone have everyone close but have no one actually know anything about them? It was almost as if he made people forget to ask. Thinking about the exhaustion she always felt after being caught in his magnetism, she could understand why. He was exciting to talk to, he was so pretty, and he made you feel good about yourself when you were there. But when you walked away, you wanted to curl up in a ball and either cry or sleep. She was disappointed that her efforts had failed, but was even more curious to see what details Cat and Evelyn had discovered about him.

THEY CAUGHT UP WITH each other after class. Drama club was supposed to start at 4:30, and they'd decided to stay and meet in the library instead of going home. It would be largely empty at that time of day and the first meeting of Drama would be on the stage in the gym, so they likely wouldn't be disturbed if people started to come in early.

Evelyn threw her bag into a chair and slumped down into one beside it, frustrated.

"Did you guys find anything? This guy's like a fart in the wind!"

Vanessa agreed with her assessment.

"Pretty much a big fat nothing. No one knows anything and don't even know that they don't know! He hasn't had any dates as far as people know, no one knows who his family is, or anything about his past before he moved to town. It's like he appeared one day just like this and that's all anyone knows. What did you get?"

Evelyn looked dejected.

"All I could find was some property tax papers and his address. No mention of parents or siblings, and nothing online. We do know that the night of the accident Robert had been seen leaving his house after practice, and Cat, you said something about an old woman?"

Cat nodded.

"Yeah, when I was in hospital there was a woman named Dorothy who said she'd bumped into a boy, then woken up in hospital with everyone thinking she'd had a stroke."

Evelyn thought for a minute.

"Do you know where she lives?"

Cat shook her head no, but then had an idea.

"You could ask your mom? She probably knows her last name, maybe she could find out? It would be great if we could find her and ask her questions."

Evelyn agreed, but cautioned them.

"Sounds good. Mom's working tonight, and she may or may not be able to divulge that kind of information, even if she knows what it is. I'll try to catch her when she gets home in the morning and ask her then."

Cat was disappointed. She'd been hoping they'd be able to find some information on Declan, even a small detail that would help her figure out what he was going to do. And even more worrisome was that if he was the vessel, who was he working for and what was he carrying? It meant he might not be the big evil that she'd envisaged, but merely a bit player in the larger game. If that was true, how scary was the big guy?

She was so new to her powers and this world of strangeness that she wasn't sure how to use her own abilities, let alone find out what someone else's did. She knew what Evelyn could do, to an extent, which was basically like really good common sense that had been jacked up. She knew Vanessa was supposed to have powers, but didn't know what they were, or even if they would be useful. Vanessa herself had no idea what to look for. There were too many variables, and Cat didn't like it.

She looked at her watch, and sighed.

"Hey, guys, we should probably get going. It's almost 4:30 now, the meeting will be starting soon."

Vanessa and Evelyn packed up, and the trio walked apprehensively towards their new, fun group activity.

*Drama with the Devil, anyone?*

Drama club was pretty much the same as drama class, but more organized than Cat had anticipated. The teacher was there, and because it was such a large town event, almost half the high school had turned up. Hence the gym, Cat thought. Most of the people wouldn't be acting, but the organizers needed props, costumes, lighting, sound, and everything else that was required for a large production.

"No one's ever turned down if they offer to help, although they may end up moving scenery if they show no other skill set," Evelyn whispered in response to Cat's stunned expression.

Once again, *A Midsummer Night's Dream* was the topic, as it had been agreed the previous year as the spring production. It was almost December, but generally they needed the whole five months to practice, make the sets, advertise, and all the other details that went into a play of this size. Vanessa, as the actress in the family, planned to try out for a lead role. Both Evelyn and Cat preferred to do behind the scenes work. Evelyn likely would end up the stage manager, thought Cat, with a grin, and then realized sadly that she'd end up moving scenery.

Cat continued to watch and listen carefully. Declan had arrived and his aura remained the dark, black hole of invisibility that she'd seen the last time she'd been close to him. Wisps of silver wafted towards him, unnoticed by anyone else. She watched as surreptitiously as she could, fascinated. She wondered how he did it, and why he didn't have an aura himself.

*Does that mean he had no soul? Is that why other auras go toward him?*

Hoping the book her grandma had written had more answers, Cat reluctantly turned her attention back towards the drama teacher. By the end of the meeting, she'd somehow volunteered to paint trees with Evelyn and a few other tenth graders she knew vaguely by sight. Vanessa, of course, had joined a project with Declan and some of the other twelfth graders. From the sounds of it, the usual procedure was to make the sets first, and get as much done before Christmas break as possible. Then in January after exams, they'd hold auditions for the show, and continue to prepare everything else while the actors practiced their lines.

The meeting broke up at six, and since Vanessa had the new car, they drove Evelyn home. She promised to ask her mom in the morning if she remembered the name of the woman from the hospital and Cat planned to spend the evening reading her grandma's journal. Vanessa still wasn't sure what she believed, but agreed it was strange that she couldn't get anything out of Declan or anyone else, and promised to stick to him like glue at school, with breaks, of course, so that she didn't get sucked dry with exhaustion. Nothing motivated her more than a challenge, a trait all of the girls had in common. Cat would have felt bad for Declan if she hadn't been so scared she wouldn't figure out what was happening before the badness, whatever it was, went down.

THE NEXT FEW WEEKS passed quickly. They started to hang out after class, using studying as an excuse. Usually, Evelyn came over to their house on nights that Marie-Jean was working so she could stay for supper. It had taken awhile to obtain the name of the woman Cat had met in hospital, but they finally had it, and planned on trying to find and talk to her on Saturday. Well, at least Cat did. The other two girls thought it would be better if she went alone, to be be less intimidating. Naturally, Cat promised to share all the details afterward.

Vanessa sat next Declan as often as possible to ask him questions throughout classes, but found it hard to stay awake and focus when she did. It helped to have Cat available and able to heal her. Whenever she was feeling really down or tired, Vanessa made a point of seeing Cat at class breaks or at lunch time. With some persistence, she'd managed to find out more than the basics everyone already knew. She'd discovered where he lived, that he apparently threw great parties according to some of the other girls in her class, he was well liked, played basketball, and was into drama club. She'd also found out that he volunteered at the local seniors centre which she found alarming considering Cat's theory that he could suck the life out of people.

When she'd told Cat, she'd been furious.

"You mean to tell me he spends time volunteering in a place where people are expected to have strokes and die? That's really convenient and deeply sick."

Cat decided on the spot she'd volunteer too, to see if he was doing the soul sucking/aura stealing thing while he was there and to try and reverse the damage. With Christmas coming up, it was the perfect opportunity to get involved with some of the seasonal activities that the school participated in.

Their first Saturday at the centre was with the school as part of an open invitation to anyone in the drama club that was interested in singing Christmas carols. They all went, even though only Vanessa could actually sing. Cat was well aware that her voice was horrible, so planned to lip sync while watching the audience, and Declan, if he was there. She'd also packed the school yearbook with Declan's picture from the year before, which had been provided by Evelyn, so that she could have Dorothy identify whether the boy who'd caused her 'stroke' was Declan after she was done singing.

When they arrived, the school set up in a large room with a piano, rows of chairs and plenty of empty space. The music teacher was in charge, and they'd been forced to practice during the Wednesday drama club meeting that week, which they'd all found extremely painful. Cat looked around as the residents filed in. She saw some of the brightest, most amazing auras, as well as some that were dark, dingy and slimy in nature. Some of the worst appearing ones were people she saw who had one sided weaknesses, or appeared to be almost zombie-slow in their movements. She wondered if Declan had been the cause, or if it had been damage from their lives that had brought them to this place and that state of existence.

As they sang, Cat concentrated on the warmth in her chest, and sent it out to those who appeared to be dull and broken. As the singing continued, she concentrated hard on people with sad, dark auras, and began to see them lighten up, slowly at first, then with more impressive changes. A few of the people who'd initially looked drowsy or inattentive began to sit up straighter, looking around with wonder at the singers and the decorations.

*It's working*!

Cat was ecstatic. Finally, she was starting to be able to heal without touch. It was still limited to one person at a time, as she couldn't focus on more than that yet, but she was hoping that would change with practice.

Too soon the singing was over. Declan hadn't showed, which was probably for the best, but as Cat looked around the room she could tell things were generally brighter and better. Vanessa and Evelyn had joined the other students in helping take the residents over to the dining room. The plan was to sing, then hand out cookies, tea, and coffee. As Cat watched, she noted that almost all the auras were bright now, in beautiful combinations of silver and gold. She noticed many of the people appeared to have more energy. Once again, she was tired, but more like she'd just been on a nice trail run, not tired like when she first started trying to heal. Her grandma had been right about so much already, she just wished she had more information with respect to who and what Declan was.

She had Dorothy's address, and had planned to leave and go over right after snack time was over. Vanessa and Evelyn would meet her back at the house when she was done. Cat caught the other girls eyes. They nodded then she slipped out of the room carrying her backpack with the yearbook and exited the building. It was a short walk from the centre and soon she was at the address that Marie-Jean had provided. Cat took a deep breath, then knocked on the door of a small, nondescript, but pleasant looking house.

"Hello?"

The white haired woman Cat remembered from the hospital stood in the entrance.

"Um, Hi. You don't know me but... "

Cat's words were cut off by a big hug that enveloped her in a cloud of roses.

"Oh, my dear! Of course I remember you! How could I forget? You saved my life!"

Cat let out her breath. This might be easier then she'd thought.

"Can I come in? I want to ask you some questions, about the first day you went to the hospital. It could be important to something I'm trying to figure out."

Dorothy stepped back.

"Of course! Come in, come in already, and shut the door. It's cold out today."

She shooed Cat into the entryway as she continued talking.

"I thought I'd never see you again my dear! What a nice surprise. I thought you were just a dream!"

Cat followed her into the house, walking into a neatly organized floral patterned living room.

"I was just making tea, would you like some?"

Cat shook her head.

"No, thank you, but I'd love a glass of water, if I may?"

Dorothy smiled and nodded, gesturing for Cat to sit. She waited on the couch while Dorothy went to the kitchen, trying to think about how to best ask questions to get information when Dorothy returned.

"Do you remember in the hospital, you told me you'd ran into a boy? And after that, you'd been broken? Those were the words you used, which I think is interesting."

Dorothy nodded.

"Yes, I was out walking my dog, Bootsie, a little grey and white Bichon."

She looked sad as she remembered.

"He unfortunately didn't make it, I was told he was hit by a car. He, the boy, came out of nowhere, and all I remember was he touched me and looked right at me. His eyes were so dark, like night had fallen. It was cold and dark in there and felt like a lake, like jumping into a cold lake. And then I blacked out and woke up with everyone telling me that I'd had a stroke. And then I was broken, until you found me."

Dorothy took a sip of tea and smiled at her.

"I've never been so happy in my life as I was the day I saw you. I thought you were an angel from heaven. For the first time in months, I felt warm inside again, like I'd made it back into the sun. And then I could talk, and walk, and now I live on my own again."

Cat blushed at her gratitude.

"I'm glad I could help. I'd never done anything like that before. I kind of found out some things about myself when I was in the hospital too."

She asked her a few more questions, but as nice as Dorothy was, and as helpful as she tried to be, she couldn't remember any details. Cat finally pulled out the yearbook with Declan's picture, and Dorothy pointed at him.

"That's him. He's the one who did it to me."

It confirmed what Cat had suspected. Step one was complete. Now the challenge was to find out where he came from, and what he was up to.

# CHAPTER ELEVEN
# THE CHRISTMAS PARTY

CAT AND THE OTHERS began to get increasingly frustrated as the next few weeks passed. Their inability to find out anything about Declan was complete on all fronts. Just when they had almost given up hope for the year, Declan invited the entire high school over for a Christmas party before winter break. Well, it was actually just the drama club and the basketball team who were invited, but it worked out to pretty much anyone who wanted to go could go, since that list included almost everyone.

Finally they had a chance to get into his house and look around, and hopefully find something useful. They all planned to go, of course, but would split up and each take a different role. Vanessa would keep Declan in sight at all times, and give the others a heads up if he was coming. Cat and Evelyn were on snoop patrol, separately if possible, to double the chance of discovering something.

"Does this make me look fat?"

Vanessa asked, as she tried on another shirt with her jeans.

Cat looked up briefly.

"No," she said, bored.

It was about the fifth shirt Vanessa had tried on in the previous 20 minutes, and as far as Cat was concerned, they all looked the same. Just then, the door bell rang.

"Finally!"said Cat, as she rolled her eyes and sprang up to get the door.

It was Evelyn.

"You guys ready yet?" she said, "The party's already started."

"Just waiting for Princess Vanessa to decide what she will dazzle the audience in," Cat said, mischievously.

Vanessa came down the stairs, scowling at her sister.

"I'm ready. Let's just go, okay?"

THEY PULLED INTO THE street where Declan lived and could see the street was packed with cars. The large brown and white Victorian style house was brightly and festively lit, appearing to be right out of an English country Christmas story.

"Are you guys ready?"

Cat felt nervous, and was second-guessing their half-baked plan.

"I guess so," said Vanessa. "You may need to come and spell me for a bit. I love these parties usually, but I think it's going to be exhausting this time. It's crazy how having my soul removed makes me feel so tired."

Cat nodded.

"We'll go in together, but after we find him I'll head upstairs, and Evelyn, you look around the main floor. Sound like a plan?"

Cat didn't like the idea of splitting up, but time was of the essence.

"I can do that," Evelyn replied, nodding at her confidently.

Girding themselves for a battle of sorts, the girls walked into the house. Cat looked around the room, recognizing several people from class. The party seemed typical for what she'd expect from a high school event. There was probably some alcohol somewhere, but nothing overt, likely hidden in a punch bowl somewhere. There was loud music, a Christmas tree, and people clustered in various small groups talking. As Cat shifted into her other vision, the people present were even brighter than the Christmas lights around them. Happy, glowing lights were all she could see, until she scanned the room and the darkness pooled in one of the corners.

It reminded her of old horror movies from the 1950's, the way the darkness seemed to menace and loom. She almost expected to hear a creaking door and scary music, but when she switched her vision back, the normal, innocent and perfect appearing golden boy, Declan Boyer, was what she saw instead. She watched as he smiled and chatted with everyone, and noticed that more than one female appeared enthralled with him, sitting closely beside him in order to hear whatever pearls of wisdom dropped from his mouth. Damn. He really was attractive. She felt a little robbed that she didn't get a chance to enjoy him the way others did. He was the best of everything, except the one little flaw related to how he stole souls and maybe killed people.

*Oh well, no one's perfect, right?*

She snorted to herself, thinking how many women would still go for him, even if they knew about his flaw. Especially given that the house was very sweet. It looked expensive, but in an understated way. She was pretty sure some of the artwork on the walls was original, and the furniture didn't look cheap. She turned her attention to the furnishings of the room around her.

*Even if I hadn't planned on snooping to get info about Declan, I might have anyways because it's so swanky in here.*

For the first time, Cat was looking forward to her mission. She turned her head to look at Evelyn, who was looking around the room, obviously having the same thought, as she mouthed 'Sheeeeeeet' to her when she caught her eye. Vanessa just winked at them, flipped her hair over one shoulder, and turned her personality on high as she walked over to the group where Declan was conversing.

Cat and Evelyn watched Vanessa as she walked, and literally lit up that part of the room. Vanessa could put out wattage like no one Cat had ever met before, when she wanted to. She almost seemed to glow. Cat flipped over to her other sight, and was startled to see that Vanessa actually *was* glowing, shooting out sparks to those nearest to her, which created an effect like fire, catching on the tinder of the auras of people nearby, creating a bigger fire. She was the opposite of Declan, Cat realized, who drew others toward him and gave nothing back.

The people near Vanessa were actually glowing brighter than before she'd walked over, and Cat was horrified to see that Declan had repositioned himself closer to her. Cat watched as her sister's bright aura sparks disappeared into his blackness, and he appeared more content, like a cat lapping up a rich cream.

*Crap, we need to move fast!*

"Don't take long, Evelyn," Cat whispered. "I think we only have like 15 minutes tops before something bad happens to Vanessa."

Evelyn nodded, and disappeared into the crowd while Cat weaved through people in the other direction, looking for a set of stairs.

She arrived at a set of small, plain stairs tucked into the kitchen, likely designed to be used by servants, and looked around to make sure she wasn't being watched before swiftly walking up the steps. She planned to say she was looking for a bathroom if she was caught, but was hoping to avoid conversation if possible. At the top, she found herself in a back hallway, with what appeared to be linen closets around her. The floor was plain wood, and the walls were painted a muted colour.

She continued down the hall. She hadn't seen any maids or other staff, so assumed there wasn't anyone living there, but she didn't want to be caught unprepared. She flipped to her other sight as she walked and didn't see anyone in the darkness.

*Handy that I don't need a light to see people. Although it won't help me not trip and fall over anything in the dark.*

That thought caused her to watch her step more carefully. She opened the first door, finding only a bare room. She opened a few more and saw nothing exciting, until she got to the fourth door, where she saw some old papers sitting out on a desk.

It appeared to be a Butler's office or something similar as she looked around. She noticed an area where silver may have been polished, complete with what looked like polishing equipment, but there was no silver. There was also a small wooden desk with a hutch. She opened a few drawers before finding a small flat narrow drawer that opened, and pulled out a sheaf of papers. The writing was odd and seemed browned with age. She looked closer, wishing she'd brought a flashlight after all, although the girls had agreed it would have looked suspicious if they'd been caught.

The paper appeared to be a deed. She could barely make out the name on the papers, but it looked like it said Declan Boyen. Weird, she thought, almost the same name but different spelling. She took a quick rifle through the rest of the papers, but nothing else stood out. The year on the deed was 1876 and she filed away the date for later. If it was the same person, that would make Declan much older than she'd imagined.

She put everything back exactly how she'd found it and carefully peered into the hallway with her aura-vision, before continuing into the passage. She could hear music from the party below and kept her aura sight on to avoid running into someone unexpectedly. As she progressed, she noticed that the hallway had changed and was much nicer, with thicker carpeting and a pretty damask wallpaper. The doors were now a rich dark wood, instead of muted paint.

She entered the next room and was impressed by the books she saw on the shelves. The room had the kind of smell associated with old books and libraries, and the statues in the room looked very old. She pulled one of the books out to look at it more closely. *The Canterbury Tales.* She pulled out another book of Shakespeare's sonnets, first edition. She was impressed.

*What the heck? How do they have all these books? They look ancient!*

Thinking of that brought her back to the task at hand. People who paid for expensive stuff. Parents.

*I must see if I can find a bedroom or something with personal items. Unless ... he's the only person who lives here?*

With that new idea whispering quietly in her mind, she looked around the library again. Other than what seemed to be an impressive collection of old books and furniture, there wasn't anything personal in the room. She reluctantly pulled herself away from the amazing book collection and left the room, walking along the long hallway again, cautiously opening each door she came to.

Most had the appearance of spare bedrooms or sitting rooms. After what felt like a hundred doors, she finally opened one to a room that looked lived in. She scanned the room, and saw a school backpack. Finally! She went inside and opened a door on the wall and examined the closet, seeing a collection of clothes one would expect a teenage male to wear. Next, she went through the desk, but was disappointed by it's mundane contents.

She gazed around the room, trying to think, searching for anything out of place. *Where would I put things that were special to me but I didn't want anyone to see?*

Her gaze fell to the bed. It was an elegant four-poster with curtains and it was also very high off the ground. With a sigh, she bent over and flipped up the bed skirt. Underneath, she saw an old, handcrafted wooden box. It wasn't locked, which she thought was odd, but then again, maybe Declan wasn't worried about anyone finding his room.

She opened the box and inside was another collection of papers. Mostly written in English, they seemed to go back several centuries. One looked like it was French, and another maybe was written in German. She scanned an English one, and saw it again featured the first name Declan, but the last name was Byers. It looked like a birth announcement, but the year was 1645. She looked through the others, and saw one that had the year 1178 on it, and the date June 17th. She also saw another date, 1196, and a death announcement for a man and a woman. It looked as though it had been tacked on a board at one time. The oldest two appeared to be made out of a fabric of some type, with corners that had rolled and browned with time. She handled them carefully with a sense of awe.

*This should be in a museum.*

Suddenly, she heard voices. Cat rolled everything back up as quickly and carefully as she could, placing the items gingerly back in the box. The voices stopped just outside the door, and Cat looked around.

*Crap, where to hide?*

She decided on the closet, as it had been closed when she came in and hopefully there wasn't anything in there that would be needed.

"Just a minute, okay? I think it's in my backpack."

From her hiding place, Cat heard Declan's voice as he came into the room.

"Sure, no prob."

She heard what sounded like Vanessa outside the room.

*Oh crap, oh crap, oh crap!*

Cat said a little prayer under her breath that he wouldn't notice that someone had been in the room. Luckily, whatever Vanessa had done or said worked and Declan left the room shortly after he'd come in. Cat counted to 20 before she slowly opened the closet door and looked around. No auras, no sounds of footsteps. Cat went back the way she had come, down the hallway back to the servant stairs, and managed to get to the bottom without anyone noticing.

She went back into the main party area and mingled with a few people she'd met at school. It actually seemed like a nice party, if she could forget it was being held by a potentially evil serial killer. Cat tried to enjoy herself with the music and the snacks, but continued to worry until she saw Evelyn appear, none the worse for her trip.

She came over and gave her a wink.

"How's the party going?"

Cat gave a half shrug.

"It's okay. Have you seen Vanessa?"

Evelyn shook her head.

"Nope."

"Crap," Cat said. "Well, at least I see Declan over there, so we know she's not with him."

Strangely, that didn't make her feel any better. A feeling of horror washed down her back when she remembered the last time she'd heard her sister with Declan, and now she was nowhere to be seen.

"Let's go look for her, okay? I'll feel a whole lot better if I can see she's alright. We were gone a long time."

Evelyn agreed.

"Sure. I don't like not seeing her in the open either."

Cat said goodbye to the people she'd been standing with and they started to weave their way through the crowd.

They finally found Vanessa in the back yard, sitting alone on a bench, appearing to be peacefully looking into the garden from behind. Cat looked at her, and was appalled when she came around and saw her sister's face. She had the same look that Cat had seen on Dorothy at first, dazed and with slumped shoulders. She rushed over and touched Vanessa's face and after a few seconds, Vanessa looked up at her, confused. She tried to speak, but could only slur her words a first.

Cat could see how someone would think she was drunk or worse. When she examined at her aura it was awful. It was dark, slimy, and shattered looking.

*What the hell had he done to her?*

The warmth that filled Cat's chest felt a lot more like anger, but she tried to calm herself and focused on healing her sister. This time, she put both hands on Vanessa, not wanting to take the chance of not being able to heal her. She knew she was stronger when she added a physical presence. She felt the warmth flow toward her sister and began to see the shimmer coming back to her aura. Evelyn watched silently, not saying anything, as she knew Cat needed to concentrate.

Finally, Vanessa blinked and looked at her sister.

"Hey. Wow. That felt really, really bad."

Evelyn came closer, looking relieved.

"What happened?"

Vanessa looked confused again.

"Well, we were talking with everyone, then I mentioned something about the play. He said he wanted to show me his copy, something about it being an original. I just figured he was bragging, but I wanted to make sure he didn't bump into either of you somewhere you shouldn't be, so I went with him."

She stopped, shaking her head as though trying to jog her memory.

"The next thing I know, I'm here with you guys."

Cat gave her a huge hug.

"I'm so sorry I didn't get here sooner. Do you have any idea what he did to you?"

Vanessa shook her head again.

"No. I feel okay now and nothing hurts physically. I remember feeling like I was falling into darkness and I'd never feel warm again, but just when I got really scared, it was gone. I was gone, I was nothing. I just was sort of...drifting away. Here, but gone. Then the warmth came and I could see daylight, and the most beautiful feeling of lightness in my body, and I was whole and here you are."

Evelyn looked at Cat and smiled wryly.

"That's a pretty kick-ass ability you have by the way."

Cat blushed in the dark, grateful they couldn't see her face. She hated it when she turned red.

Vanessa laughed shakily.

"Well, if I had any doubts before about Declan, I can tell you they're gone now. He's a completely evil bastard in my books."

"What do you want to do now, Cat?" Evelyn asked, looking at Vanessa with a concerned expression.

"We could just leave out the back way, or should we go back in? Which would look more suspicious?"

Vanessa stood up slowly, and Cat felt how her sister looked. She was wiped and was done with the party.

"Let's sneak off. I need to go to bed."

Vanessa agreed.

"Hey, Evelyn, do you feel up to driving? I'm still feeling a little punky."

A flicker of excitement crossed Evelyn's face. She'd just gotten her license and rarely got to drive her mom's car.

"On it!"

The sisters walked out of the garden supporting each other, Evelyn in front with the keys. They left unnoticed by the rest of the party goers.

They'd previously decided to have a sleep-over at the McLean house in the living room, so they got out the sleeping bags and set up quietly. Cat brought chips and pop from the kitchen, and set up the Xbox. It was still early after all, and it *was* a sleep over.

"What did you find out, Cat? Anything worth all the effort?"

Vanessa slumped over the ottoman, eating a bag of dill pickle chips upside down.

"I'm don't know. I think Declan is a heck of a lot older than 18 though, that's for sure. I found papers with several dates, but the oldest one goes back to 1178, June 18th, to be precise."

When the girls looked at her, confused, Cat hesitated before continuing.

"I think it looked like it may be his birth announcement."

Evelyn shook her head.

"That can't be. He would be, like, 900 if that's true."

Cat agreed.

"Actually, About 840. But almost."

Vanessa protested.

"How's that even possible?"

Cat thought for a minute.

"Well, if he steals souls, maybe he stays young from taking them? Although, from what I've read in the journal Grandma left me, it doesn't sound like he's working alone." Cat leaned forward.

"What if he's stealing souls for someone else? And whoever that is keeps him young in exchange?"

As she thought about it, Cat felt in her bones that the possibility was real. It felt right. Evelyn and Vanessa sat quietly, munching on chips, thinking about what she'd said.

"This is so out of my league," Evelyn said, matter-of-factly, eating another chip.

The girls talked a little longer before the adrenaline wore off and they decided to call it a night. Each girl laid in the darkness, quiet but with open eyes for a long time. Evelyn was overwhelmed, experiencing things beyond her comprehension and frustrated at her lack of ability to see more.

Vanessa was still shaken from her near-soulless experience. Although she hadn't admitted it to the others, she was still feeling tainted by darkness.

Cat had a hard time falling asleep, even though she was tired. She kept replaying what she'd seen that night and wondered how it was all possible. A thought suddenly struck her. If Declan was as old as the papers she'd found suggested, and he could steal souls, what did it mean if Cat herself could regenerate souls? Did that mean she would be like a traditional phoenix, and rise from her own ashes? Did that mean she would never die? She lay awake for a long, long time, questions swirling in her head.

# CHAPTER TWELVE
## REVELATIONS

CHRISTMAS BREAK PASSED with a whole lot of nothing for the girls, but they made an attempt to do some research in the library and at home. They eventually gave up due to family obligations over the holidays, but promised that they'd each keep searching online whenever they had a chance. Vanessa was more than a little obsessed with trying to find Declan's weakness. She was still furious at how he'd put her into that broken, dirty state, and wanted to make him pay for it. Cat almost felt bad for him. She knew how single-minded her sister could be, and it wasn't fun to be on her bad side. Cat searched long and hard for information about the dates she'd found, but because it was so far into the past, it was difficult to find anything other then vague historical accounts that may or may not be related.

The day before the break was over, Cat found an interesting article with the date June 18, 1178. She wasn't sure how or if it applied to Declan, but it looked like the kind of thing that would be considered 'an omen' of something coming. As she read, she felt cold trickle down her spine and was both fascinated and repulsed. It seemed like too big of a coincidence not to be related, but as for how it could help them, she had no idea. With nothing else to go on, she went with her gut, which was screaming for her to pay attention, and read the article.

"'On the night of June 18th, just past sunset, a group of five monks watched as the moon was hit by a meteor. A flaming torch sprang up, spewing out over considerable distance, fire, rocks and sparks. Meanwhile, the body of the moon which was below writhed, as if it were in anxiety, and to put it in the words of those who reported it to me and saw it with their own eyes, the moon throbbed like a snake. Afterwards, it resumed its proper state. This was repeated a dozen times or more, the flame assuming various twisting shapes at random and then returning to normal. Then after these transformations the moon took on a blackish shape.'"

She scrolled to what the description was about, and realized it was from what historians thought was the formation of the Giardano Bruno moon crater. It was the same date as what she thought was Declan's birth, and the description sounded to her like fire versus darkness, which could be important to the current situation. The question was how.

So far, all Cat had was a theory and a whole bunch of speculation. Declan was probably born June 18, 1178. He appeared to be 18, but was likely over 800 years old. According to her grandma's journal, he was a vessel for something, or a tool for someone else. This probably meant he wasn't the biggest evil in play, just the one they knew about. Now it appeared he may have been born during the night of an asteroid hitting the moon, which would have been a huge deal in the Middle Ages in terms of magic or witchcraft or whatever superstition people believed in at that time. Or maybe it wasn't superstition after all.

He could suck energy out of people, but she wasn't sure about a full soul. Most of what she'd seen and heard made her believe he could only take part, as people didn't die immediately, like she'd expect if he could take an entire soul. Even though he didn't seem able to take the whole thing, at least one death that they knew of was directly tied to him. Robert wouldn't have died if he hadn't been at Declan's, Cat had no doubt of that. She wondered how many more people were dead because of him, and redoubled her efforts to find a way to beat him.

JANUARY WAS ALWAYS a big pile of cold suck as far as Cat was concerned. It was snowy and grey, she couldn't run outside without breaking her leg on the ice, and holidays were over until spring break. School wasn't remotely keeping her interest, and other than an unproductive but ongoing search for information on Declan, they only had drama club to help them pass the time. No wonder almost everyone's involved, Cat thought gloomily. There's nothing else to do in this town.

At least they had moved past just planning and talking she thought, while she put another coat of paint on what was supposed to be a tree. Cat and Evelyn were on prop duty, both having decided they had no interest in being a face on stage. Evelyn, as expected, was supervising, more unofficially than actually appointed, but she pretty much told the prop group what to do. And the funny thing was, no one ever argued with her. It was nice to have someone tell you what to do sometimes. Less thinking was involved and that was good, especially when your mind wanted to stay busy with other things.

The play was coming along. Most of the scenery had been completed and costumes had been designed but weren't done, as they had to wait for actor sizing in order to fit them properly. Auditions for the play had begun the week before, starting with the small roles and working up to the bigger ones, possibly to build tension, Cat assumed. Declan got the role of Robin Goodfellow and Vanessa had tried for and won the role of Hermia. Cat was unhappy because of her sister's proximity to Declan in the play, but he hadn't done or said anything since his party to alarm them. They'd been watching him closely, and Vanessa had worked hard to be friendly with him but also keep her distance.

He hadn't appeared to notice anything different, but Cat wondered if he'd been surprised when he'd seen Vanessa recovered to her normal self. Or if he wasn't as connected to the souls he stole as she'd thought. Maybe it was like breathing and you didn't notice it unless you ran out of air?

*It's not like I took her soul back from him either. I healed Vanessa from my own soul and regenerated it, so maybe he still has her energy and that's why he didn't notice. Man, I almost need a physics degree in subatomic particles or something to understand soul transfer energy.*

"Like they've ever studied it," she huffed under her breath.

Evelyn looked over curiously and Cat realized her irritability was noticeable to others.

"Sorry", she mouthed.

Evelyn nodded back then continued painting.

Cat found herself watching Declan again, using her aura-vision now. It was amazing to her how he pulled light from other people in. He didn't even look like it was something he was aware of. He just stood there, talking and pleasant, siphoning energy from others who appeared none the wiser. She did notice that he rarely seemed to touch people, and when he did, it was only for brief periods of time. Cat realized if just being close to people drained them, he probably ran the risk of sucking them dry if contact was more intimate or prolonged, which would get him noticed eventually. Wow, that would totally suck for trying to have a relationship with anyone.

Cat briefly felt sad for him, living 800 years without anyone to love or be close to him. What would be worth that? If he'd been born in 1178, that meant he'd been human at least once, assuming he wasn't now, which she wasn't clear on. 800 years without any parents, siblings, love interests or close friends. How awful. Cat suddenly felt better about her life. Being 16 and passing through was one thing, but staying 18 for centuries must have a special kind of crappiness that went beyond anything she could imagine.

Cat realized she'd been approaching this from the perspective that Declan was all bad. What if he wasn't? Granted, he was stealing soul energy from people and was likely a murderer, so not a model human being by any standards, but what if he was trapped here as well? What if he'd been born normal, and something happened to him to keep him

18 for life and give him this ability? After all, Cat only got her powers at 16, and was completely normal before the accident. Well, not completely, she admitted to herself. She'd always had feelings about things. What if that's what her grandma had meant about him being the vessel? That he took souls and held them for another, bigger evil?

With this idea in mind, Cat looked at Declan, really looked at him. His face was pleasant, attractive even. He had good teeth and no obvious scarring. When she looked at his eyes they were dark and hard to read. He looked bored, if she really examined the little emotion she saw in them. And why wouldn't he be? He was 800 years old in grade 12.

*I'd probably stab myself in the eye with a fork.*

So why was he here? And why now? Why would you be in grade 12 when you were 800 if you didn't have to? Maybe that was the key. Maybe he did have to be here now, for some reason, and be an 18 year old in school in the middle of America. Maybe he needed to take a lot of souls for some reason, a whole boat load. Disturbed, Cat turned her attention back to her artwork, planning to discuss the idea later with Vanessa and Evelyn.

THAT NIGHT, CAT FOUND herself dreaming. It was almost as though she'd fallen through Alice's rabbit hole into a dark wonderland. It was night in her dream, but with a huge full moon that lit up the sky with an eerie glow. A small cottage appeared in front of her, a little run down, with holes in the thatched roof and dead flowers outside the door. She saw a light in a window without glass and went over to look through it. She was surprised to see Declan inside the house and he looked sick. He was laying on a pallet on the floor with nasty swellings on his neck, and he looked flushed with fever. His eyes were glassy, and he was coughing.

She felt with eerie certainty that he was alone and dying. He appeared scared, but when a swirling darkness presented inside the doorway across from her view point and shaped itself into a human form, he didn't even flinch. He lay there listlessly while he watched with exhaustion until the figure spoke.

"Declan Boyer. I am here to make you an offer."

Declan looked at him, and then coughed with a deep, racking sound, spitting blood into cupped hands that had been covering his mouth.

"What offer? Who are you?"

His voice was so weak and quiet that Cat could hardly hear it.

The figure spoke again in a deep voice, a hood shrouding his face from view, but long bony hands waving away his question.

"You need not concern yourself with who I am. I offer you the chance to live. And in exchange, you must do something for me."

Declan watched mutely. The figure paused, then continued to speak.

"I will give you life everlasting. And you will give me your soul in return, in addition to a tribute every 117 years."

This sick and weak appearing Declan looked confused.

"Are you Satan? Come to tempt me?" he asked in disbelief.

The figure laughed coldly, a sound full of menace.

"I am nothing like the Satan your foolish Bible wants you to think exists. I am so much more. However, the choice is yours. You will die if I leave here, within days at most, following your poor departed parents and most of those you know. If this is your wish, I shall of course leave you to it. If you would prefer to know and see more, and live longer with the power I can bestow upon you, you only have to give me that which you do not use and gather more of the same in tribute."

The shrouded figure paused, waiting silently for Declan's reply.

Sick Declan did look moribund, almost swaying with the effort to sit up and talk. Cat could almost see the internal debate, but his decision didn't take long.

"I'm not ready to die. I'm only eighteen. What is it you would have me do?"

The dark figure swept his skeletal fingers majestically, and an image appeared on the cottage wall of a healthy Declan from another time. He was talking to people with the light from their auras being drawn towards him. "This. Only this, until 117 years have passed. Simply by existing, you will draw others towards you. If they die while you are in possession of pieces of their soul, they will come to me."

Declan asked the logical question.

"What happens in 117 years?"

The figure laughed mirthlessly.

"A tribute. You must collect a number of souls at one time, on the anniversary of your immortality, to earn another 117 years. You will do this with your presence, and I will collect them from you. If you fail, you shall forfeit your life to me and you will die."

Declan coughed again, this time so hard a spray of blood came out from between his fingers and his face went white. A scared expression crossed his face, and he nodded mutely.

The figure moved to the pallet where Declan still reclined, and brought a parchment and quill out from underneath his robes.

"You must sign here to seal the deal."

Declan took the quill with surprising alacrity, signed, and the figure moved his arm and the parchment vanished as quickly as it had appeared.

"You shall be well. One piece of advice, if I may?"

The figure tilted his head slightly.

"You may want to keep moving. People tend to notice if you aren't aging. And that can be irritating."

As suddenly as he'd appeared, the dark stranger vanished. Declan was left sitting in the room, covered with blood from his previous coughing spell, but no longer pale or with neck swelling. He looked exactly like the boy that Cat knew, 800 years into the future.

CAT SAT BOLT UPRIGHT in her bed, breathing heavily. It took her a minute to realize she was back in her own bed in her room, alone. It had been so real, she felt she could have touched Declan. She'd been able to smell everything, which had been unpleasant. She wouldn't forget what that sickness had smelled like. And the Declan of that time hadn't made her feel the dark coldness of a bottomless lake. He'd been human and normal. And he'd had an aura, although it had been a very sick bile yellow with putrid green flecks.

The figure she'd seen with him had made her feel a hundred times worse than Declan had ever made her feel. It had been like ice, like the deepest, darkest, remotest reaches of space. She vaguely remembered her science teacher talking about the kelvin scale for temperature and for the first time she knew what absolute zero would feel like. Her heart still raced from the memory and she was grateful that the hooded figure hadn't turned his attention to her and also that she hadn't seen his face.

THE NEXT MORNING, CAT was more sluggish than usual getting out of bed. She kept replaying the dream in her mind, and must have been acting off, because even her distractible mom noticed.

"Are you feeling okay, dear? You look a little flushed this morning."

Cat shook her head and smiled.

"No, Mom, I'm fine. I just didn't sleep great. Too much homework I guess."

Her mom rolled her eyes.

"Please. I know you. Maybe too much reading, but you hardly ever have homework. Try to go to bed on time tonight, okay, sweetie?"

Cat nodded meekly, while Vanessa looked over at her curiously and mouthed, "what's up?"

Cat jerked her head in the direction of upstairs and gulped down her cereal.

They both went to brush their teeth and Vanessa asked the question that was burning in her mind, away from their mom's concern.

"Okay, spill. What's up? You look a little crazy today," she said, looking at her again then added, "you also may want to brush your hair again. It doesn't help you not look cray-cray at the moment."

Cat looked at herself in the mirror and tidied up her ponytail.

"Okay, Vanessa, I had the craziest dream last night. I was in Declan's memory somehow. Maybe when I healed you I took something into myself from him? I'm not sure, but I think I know more about what we might be facing."

She quickly related the story and waited to see what Vanessa thought. Her sister looked at her watch with frustration.

"Damn. We have to go. Look, I want you to tell Evelyn what happened then meet me at lunch so we can talk more."

Cat agreed, and the girls went out to meet their mom, who was waiting for them.

The day was painful to get through, mostly because Cat had something else to be excited about now. She'd managed to whisper her story to Evelyn during break, and she became equally excited. They finally met up with Vanessa after what felt like a million years to discuss it. They picked a table in a corner away from everyone else and Vanessa and Evelyn picked apart the dream, asking Cat every question they could think of.

"So it sounds like Declan takes souls just by being there, almost like a magnet or something. But every 117 years, as per your dream, he has to make a big offering somehow," Vanessa clarified.

Cat nodded, as Evelyn thought for a moment, then took out her calculator.

"So if we're doing the math right, and he was born in 1178 and died June 18th, 1196, wouldn't this be the year he needs to do the tribute?"

Cat wrinkled her nose in response.

"Unfortunately, yes. That's what worries me. It would also give us a date that this would go down, June 18th, and somewhere in town. What type of event would be big enough in this Podunk town to get the type of numbers he'd need?"

Vanessa looked both horrified and pissed off at the same time.

"Great. My first big break in a play, and it's all a sham."

Evelyn looked at her, confused.

"What do you mean?"

Vanessa crossed her arms and pouted as she answered.

"I mean, here I am learning lines and hoping for talent scouts so I don't have to go to university next year, and it doesn't matter anyways because we're all going to die on June 18th, at the opening night of the play."

Cat was stunned. She hadn't put the two dates together, but of course! It made total sense that the play would be the target. Evelyn had said it was the biggest event in town and that everyone came from around the area. Based on previous years, there could be several hundred people a night there, if not more, depending on seating arrangements. And the play this year was *A Midsummer Night's Dream,* which had mystical components. In particular, both Robin Goodfellow and the king and queen of the fairies figured prominently. It would be easy for Declan to get to the audience with one of the speeches he had to deliver. However the tribute was collected could then happen easily without any resistance.

"Oh God, Vanessa! That's it! You're completely right! June 18th, 2015 is the seventh anniversary of the 117 year tribute."

Evelyn looked pleased with the confirmation of her deduction.

"Now we have a date and a location. We just need to figure out the what, and how to stop it."

Cat groaned.

"Great. Oh well, at least we have some time to figure it out."

Vanessa and Evelyn looked at her with sympathy.

"Don't worry, sis, maybe you can have another dream. Or just wing it, that seems to work for you."

Vanessa winked at her while Cat scowled, then continued eating, seemingly unbothered by the revelation.

OVER THE FOLLOWING month, Cat, Vanessa and Evelyn continued to work together. Cat kept a close eye on the senior's centre where Declan volunteered, and tried to go on all the same days that he did with the drama group, and also by herself.. She felt he was the reason some of the residents died early and did her best to heal where and when she could without being noticed. She felt she'd made a difference, but also like she was fighting a losing battle. He was charming and people loved him. They practically gave themselves to him, the lonely elderly people even more willingly than the kids at school. And then Cat healed them, so that they could go ahead and do it all over again the next time he was there.

Vanessa monitored police records for suspicious deaths, having become close to a clerk at the local police department with her charm. Evelyn's mother acted as a pipeline to the hospital for any information on strange happenings there. Both of the girls were also doing everything they could to try to tap into any innate abilities they may have.

Evelyn already knew about her weak clairvoyance and was working with her mother to try to improve it. Vanessa was frustrated with her lack of ability, but they still had hope based on their grandma's journal that she would come into some sort of power.

Evelyn dropped her bag beside Cat during study period.

"There was another death last night."

Cat looked up sharply.

"Normal?"

Evelyn shook her head.

"Looked like natural causes, but was the same as the others. Previously normal guy, went for a walk and was found on the ground by a stranger having a seizure or something. He didn't make it. Apparently, he had a heart attack after getting to the hospital and died from that."

Cat was frustrated and angry.

"How can we let him continue to kill people when we know it's him doing this? We should be able to stop him, before the tribute."

Evelyn sighed, shrugging her shoulders.

"I know. I feel you, girl. But we still don't know how. How do you stop an immortal soulless evil bastard?"

The girls sat glumly, wrapped up in the dilemma. Now they knew what was happening, they needed to figure out how to stop it. And find out who or what was behind it all. These thoughts continued to plague them for the rest of the month, urging them on with the feeling of time running out.

# CHAPTER THIRTEEN
## THE TEACHERS

THE WEATHER HAD FINALLY begun to warm up enough for Cat to safely go outside for runs. Everyday after school, she'd head out to the park, needing to put her feet to the pavement. It always felt good to move, and it was as close to flying and freedom she ever felt. The only sensations were her feet slapping on the ground, her breath rasping in her chest, and her thoughts floating through her head. She was usually in an altered state of consciousness altogether by the time she got to the park, so she didn't notice the shimmer covering everything that day.

When she'd left the house after school it had still been light out, but it was early spring and already starting to get dark once the sun dipped behind the clouds. The trees were still leafless, not yet starting to bud, but she could suddenly smell flowers when she saw a glowing golden light coming from the forest just off the path. Curiosity outweighing her common sense for a change, Cat looked around carefully before following the light. At first, she was able to see around her, but before she knew it, the only light to guide her was the one emanating from in front of her. The trees became more twisted as Cat advanced, even more curious about what lay ahead.

The glow stopped abruptly, staying in front of a grassy hill that she didn't remember from the last time she'd come through this way. In the centre she saw a small stone carving. She took a deep breath then went over and touched it gingerly. A door that appeared to come right from the hill swung open with the sound of grinding stone. The glow now seemed to be coming from within the mound, but was a greenish-silvery light instead of the golden one that had initially lured her.

She entered slowly, feeling the temperature grow warmer as she walked, and noticed that the walls became mossy and soft to touch. The ground beneath her became fragrant and flowered with different varieties of plants, many of which she didn't recognize. Cat looked around, awed by the soft natural beauty around her. She stopped when she reached the far side of the tunnel and stepped outside, realizing that she'd somehow walked right into early summer. The sun was high in the sky and birds were chirping in trees filled with leaves and she felt uncomfortably warm.

As she turned around looking for a path to follow, she heard someone laughing. When she could finally see who it was, she saw a boy of about eight or nine with a twinkle in his eyes and large dimples in his tanned, nut brown cheeks. His hair curled in wild abandon and he was dressed in only a pair of cut off shorts, without shoes, socks or a shirt.

"Hello?" Cat asked, hesitantly.

Where was she? If this had any connection to the other weird things that had been happening she was afraid that she might have walked through a fairy door, right into the underworld itself. A little scared of what he would do, knowing creatures here were generally considered to be tricksters, Cat stood and waited, watching him cautiously.

He hopped lightly through the flowers, taking care not to bruise a single petal. He came to a stop on a tree branch, holding on with one arm and a leg, while he leaned over the side.

"Hale and well met, Lady Firebird."

He gave her a big smile and swung from the branch until he was hanging upside down like a monkey before flipping off and coming to stand beside her.

Cat smiled nervously.

"Hey. Um, hello. How are you? My name's Catherine, or Cat. May I ask what your name is?"

Cat winced inwardly. She'd always been very awkward meeting new people, and she hadn't really met anyone who was possibly non-human before so she was even more awkward than usual.

The boy laughed again, and clapped his hands in delight.

"Oh, you are a fine one then! Lovely to meet you, Miss Cat. I am called Robin, or Puck if I'm feeling spritely."

He chortled a little at his pun and Cat remembered that some people thought he was a woodland sprite as well. Cat relaxed slightly, seeing that he was in a good mood. She looked at him with her aura-vision and saw the most peculiar light. It was similar to how Declan looked with his lack of soul and the darkness that circled him, except it was as though he was wearing a tight green light instead.

"Ah, you have seen my clothing then, have you young lass? It matches the forest well, doesn't it?"

He pranced around in a big circle, putting his hands on his hips and head as he waggled around. Cat giggled in spite of herself. He looked exactly like a ridiculous young boy, not the extremely old earth spirit he actually was.

He looked at her approvingly.

"Very wise, to laugh at the jokes of the oldest of olds! You are welcome here. Come and follow me. You have much to learn and you are in need a teacher, are you not?"

"Pardon me, old one, but do you mean that you will teach me?"

Cat felt her excitement rise, but Robin simply laughed.

"Aye, and I will teach you some things, this is certain. But not everything. Because you are a firebird, you must have a firebird to show you the subtleties of your craft."

Cat felt her heart glow. At last! Finally, she'd learn what she could do. She'd be able to ask questions and get answers from someone or who was alive. As helpful as her grandma's journal had been, a lot of it was speculative and passed down through the family. Her grandma had also admitted she simply wasn't sure about much of it.

Cat followed Robin into a ring of trees just past the clearing, and saw a beautiful fiery golden bird sitting on a rock in the middle. It appeared to be bathing in the sun. The bird cocked its head and watched silently as Cat came closer.

Robin made a show of bowing to the bird, and introduced Cat with grandeur. "Madame Firebird, this is Miss Catherine McLean. She is in need of a teacher and if you could be so kind, she would like to learn how to use her powers to fight evil."

Cat jumped in surprise before shaking her head. Of course he'd know her last name and what she needed. He'd probably been watching her for a long time, if the legends about the Sidhe were correct. They didn't contact just anyone and were known to keep an eye on anyone with magical abilities. Cat turned to the firebird, bowing deeply then waiting. In all the fairy tales she'd read, one did not initiate conversation with magical beings without permission.

The bird opened its mouth and a beautiful golden voice spilled out like warm syrup.

"My child, it is good to meet you. I have been watching and I am proud of how far you've already come. If you are prepared, I can show you how to access more than you thought possible."

Cat nodded eagerly, then paused.

"Thank you so much, and I would most appreciate that, but how can I do that and stay where I am needed? If I stay here, does time not pass much faster than where I live? Would my family not miss me?"

The bird laughed, and it sounded like bells ringing.

"Oh my child, of course you cannot stay here. You will learn in your dreams at night. You have already walked out of your body before, and you should practice that as well. It was important to meet in person before we started, so I could give you this."

The Bird shook her feathers until one fell out. Robin merrily scampered over and plucked it out of the air before it touched the ground, presenting it to Cat with another deep flourishing bow.

Cat looked at the feather which was as large as a peacock's, but with the colours of a bonfire instead. She almost expected it to be hot to the touch, but it was as soft and warm as one would expect any bird feather to be. Cat looked back at her and the bird cooed softly.

"It is time for you to go back now. It is late, and you will be missed. Be careful who you tell. Your family will be a great asset in the days ahead, but it will get dark soon, and you must be cautious."

With those final words, the bird lifted its head and spread its wings, flying straight up into the sky.

Cat watched as she left, marvelling at her beauty and wishing she had some of it for herself. Robin danced in front of her, gleeful for some reason that she could only imagine.

"You have found a teacher, but has the teacher found a student?"

He cackled as he danced around.

"We must find a friend for the Sylph to keep company with, so that you are not alone out in the elements."

Cat was becoming more confused.

*Sylph? What Sylph? Isn't that like a wind spirit?*

She looked around, not seeing anyone else. Whatever Robin had meant, he was moving again, gesturing for her to follow. It was a struggle to keep up with his energetic pace, even though he stopped to dance from time to time. She finally found herself back at the same clearing where she'd emerged from the tunnel. In front of her she could see the tunnel itself. It wasn't as friendly looking on the way out, coloured in the darkness, but it was reassuring to see the large stone silently guarding the entrance.

"It's time to leave, Kitty-Cat," Robin said, sounding serious for the first time since he had come gambolling into her day. "You have much work to do between now and the summer solstice. And your companions do as well. Look to your dreams for answers, and let your friends know to look to theirs. You will find help if ever you need it and you have only to ask and it shall find you. Now go and run home to your family. May the four elements keep you safe."

He gave her a salute and vanished.

Cat turned and walked back into the tunnel, coming back out through the park where she had gone into the hill. It appeared to be nothing more than a slight swelling in the ground and the usual path was beside her. The sky had darkened to night and when she looked at her watch she realized she'd been away over three hours, although it had only felt like minutes. She ran as fast as she could all the way home. For the first time, she felt confident she'd be able to do the task set before her, and her running was joyful.

WHEN SHE ARRIVED HOME, her mother was in the kitchen, looking worried until she saw Cat walk in.

"Cat!"

She gave her a big hug, then gently pushed her back to look at her.

"Where the heck have you been?"

Her brows had knit together, and her mouth was pressed into a fine line as she waited for a response.

*Now she looks mad. Oh-oh.*

"Sorry Mom, I got a little lost in the park, and didn't realize what time it was."

Cat paused.

"Maybe if I could have a cell phone? I'd be able to call if it happens again."

Cat figured it would either get her a phone or make her mom mad about something else. Either way, it would distract her mom enough sot that she wouldn't question Cat's story.

Her mom snorted.

"I don't think so! You can have a cell phone when you can pay the bills yourself."

Cat pretended to pout.

"But Vanessa has one!"

Her mom scowled in response.

"Vanessa can drive. We want her to have one for safety. Maybe if you got your drivers license, we'd buy you one too."

*Ouch.*

Cat winced with hurt feelings.

"Thanks Mom. I wanted to get my license this year, but after the accident I had to wait, remember?"

Her mother instantly became contrite.

"Sorry, sweetie, I know you do. You can get it in the spring. It's just with that head injury the doctor wanted you to wait a little bit. It doesn't mean you won't be able to drive."

Cat shrugged, calming down.

"It's okay. It gives me more time to do other stuff right now."

Her mom patted her shoulder.

"Go wash up, and tell your sister it's time to eat."

Cat went upstairs and found Vanessa lying on her bed, reading a book about Scottish myths and legends. She'd been reading everything she could find about magic and mythical creatures, trying to understand this alternate reality they'd woken up in, as well as to figure out if she had any abilities of her own.

"Hey, Vanessa. Mom says it's time to eat," said Cat as she leaned in the doorway, stretching her legs from the run.

Vanessa looked up, and seemed relieved to see her.

"You were gone a long time. What happened? I was worried you'd ran into Declan or something."

Cat craned her neck to look down the stairs, making sure they were alone before she returned and sat on the bed.

"You totally won't believe it, but I met Robin Goodfellow today."

Vanessa leaned forward onto her elbows.

"Say what! No way! I thought he was just a story."

She looked impressed.

"Nope. He's real. I went through a weird tunnel and into what I think they call Summerland, and he was there, and looked like a kid. He took me to see a phoenix, who is supposed to do my training. Oh, Vanessa, she was so beautiful and amazing."

Cat stopped talking, looking off dreamily while remembering the firebird.

Vanessa waited impatiently for her to snap out of it, and had just opened her mouth to ask Cat a question, when they heard their mom yelling at them from the bottom of the stairs.

"You'd better tell me all about this later," said Vanessa, looking at her sternly.

"I promise." Cat said, before they headed downstairs to avoid the wrath of their mom.

The girls ate quickly, making excuses about homework, but the minute they got upstairs, Vanessa pounced.

"Okay, spill everything, Cat. Tell me what happened."

So Cat went through her story, about following the light into the tunnel, meeting Robin and the phoenix, and what they'd said about learning in her dreams.

Vanessa sighed.

"I wish I had a teacher in my dreams. I don't think I'll ever get any power, no matter what Grandma said."

She paused, thoughtfully considering her statement.

"I'm not sure whether I should be happy or sad about it."

Cat looked at Vanessa sympathetically.

"I know. It would've been a lot easier if I hadn't discovered mine. We'd just be out living our lives none the wiser. Of course, you could be dead by now because of Declan, but still."

Vanessa smiled.

"I'm very glad you got your powers. I just wish I knew if I have any."

Cat went to bed that night with anticipation, falling asleep almost immediately to her surprise. She began to dream, finding herself in the same forest in which she'd last seen the phoenix. She walked into the small clearing and in front of her was the bird, waiting gracefully on the rock.

"Hello again, my little firebird."

The melodic voice of the bird wrapped around her like the warmth of hot chocolate, and Cat sat down on a nearby log.

"Hello. Thank you for helping me."

The bird inclined her head.

"You may call me Glory. Tonight, I want to show you how to see beyond the veil, to separate the real from the surreal."

Cat nodded, eager to learn everything.

THE NIGHT PASSED QUICKLY, and Cat woke up feeling fresh and awake, which wasn't normal for her. It was as though all the practice she'd done in her dreams had recharged her. She felt amazing and couldn't wait to try the new things that Glory had shown her about auras during the coming day. She'd learned she could separate auras into different components and tell which elemental powers people possessed, even if they didn't know they had magic themselves. She was most interested to see if she could tell anything about her sisters nascent powers this way and rushed to get downstairs to look.

She practically bounced into the kitchen, earning a surprised look from both her mom and Vanessa.

"Good morning!" she chirped, while she filled her bowl with Cheerios.

Her mom laughed.

"Well, good morning, and what have you done with my daughter? Did you just find the right side of the bed for the first time?"

Cat gave her a sunny smile and sat down to eat, ignoring the good-natured jibe.

Vanessa jerked her head in the direction of the stairs and Cat nodded. She knew what that meant. She ate quickly and put her bowl in the sink before heading back to the stairs.

Vanessa had gone on ahead and was waiting in the bathroom.

"Okay, tell me. What happened last night? You're practically glowing."

Cat twirled around in a circle, hugging herself.

"I've never woken up so happy! It was great. Glory, that's her name, helped me learn more about auras. I thought colours just showed moods, but she told me that they can mean more than that. She says that I can tell who has abilities, as well as if they are sick or whatever. Everything colours a person's aura. For example, a blue tinge could mean water affinity, green for earth, and purple for air. Obviously, fire would be gold or orange."

Vanessa looked excited.

"So what does that mean? Do you see anything for me? What about Mom and Dad?"

Cat shook her head.

"Mom has sort of the happy generic gold/silver, so I don't think that she has any abilities. Dad has blue, but we already know he has a weak water magic."

Vanessa interrupted her.

"What about me? Do you see anything for me?"

Cat smiled, understanding her need to know.

"Yes, Vanessa. You have had a very strong purple colour, ever since I can remember."

Vanessa clapped her hands together.

"Finally! A direction! I wonder what that means for powers."

She looked pensive as she packed her school bag, not paying attention to Cat anymore. Cat smiled, happy she'd been able to give her sister a focus. She grabbed her bag as well and they headed downstairs.

At school they filled Evelyn in, and she brightened with excitement.

"This is good. Great, even! We're totally on the right track. My mom's helping me develop my intuition, so between you getting better at reading auras and me getting better at seeing things for what they are, we just need Vanessa to figure her deal out and then we can totally take Declan! And maybe Mr. Shadow Man to boot!"

Cat looked skeptical.

"I'd be happy just figuring out what to do about Declan. How do we take down a guy with no soul who plans on stealing the souls of a few hundred people? Possibly with an audience, if he does it mid-show like we think he will."

The other two looked deflated at this reality check, but it was impossible to completely lose the excitement of the breakthrough that had been made.

That night, Cat got ready for bed eagerly. She quickly brushed her teeth and didn't even pick up a book as she normally would have. She closed her eyes and thought of the night before. She fell asleep easily, drifting back in to the same area she'd visited before. This time, she asked the question she had promised Vanessa she would.

"I'm sorry to bother you, but can you help me with my sister? She needs to find out what her power is so she can help me. So far, we haven't been able to figure it out. We aren't sure if she even has one. She has the purple of an air adept, but hasn't had any control yet."

Cat paused, then continued.

"It's the most purple I've ever seen, so I feel like she may be strong. But she's still had no flicker of power yet."

Glory looked at her serenely.

"Your sister will be visited soon. Worry not. Now back to you. Tonight we will practice healing."

And so the night passed in lessons as the previous one had, and Cat learned, and learned.

THE DAYS PASSED WITH the girls doing as much as they could. Evelyn and Cat learned to hone their powers. Vanessa was still frustrated, but had read everything she could find about different air beings and powers. She hadn't yet figured out how to awaken her power and was upset that Cat had told her that her guide would come but that she still hadn't met them, weeks later.

It was now spring and May was beautiful, with trees in bud and flowers blooming. Vanessa had taken to walking to the park where Cat had first met Robin, in the hope that the door in the hill would be there for her, too. Cat joined her one day and the two girls took the same path. Until then, the path had stayed mundane to Vanessa. Yet on the walk that day, she noticed a new tree in the middle of other trees. It was standing alone with sprawling branches and roots and was emitting a faint green glow that was almost undetectable. Cat noticed it because of the aura, but Vanessa was the first one to be struck by it's power.

After looking at each other and taking deep breaths, the girls held hands and walked toward it. The tree must have stood twenty feet tall, its twisting branches covered with buds and birds singing in the crook. They both saw an indentation at the base of the tree and when they approached they realized it was the entrance to a tunnel. It looked small from a distance but when they got closer, it grew, becoming big enough for them to enter while crouching. They had to put their hands on the ground for balance, but the tunnel was short, and grew larger as they walked, so they were soon able straighten out.

As quickly as they'd entered they emerged into a sun-dappled clearing where dandelion puffs danced in the breeze. Vanessa scanned her surroundings, blinking at the hazy golden air, which was unlike anything she'd ever seen before. Cat looked around, expecting to see Glory or Robin. The noise of something dropping out of the tree behind them startled them. They quickly spun around and as Cat had expected, a laughing boy bounced up from beneath the branches.

"Hale and well met, Lady Firebird! How goeth the lessons?"

Robin did a few somersaults in the grass before stopping at their feet.

"Good afternoon, Robin Goodfellow. I'm well and am learning much from Glory. This is my sister, Vanessa. She's learning much as well, although sadly she hasn't discovered powers of her own as of yet."

Vanessa bowed cautiously, giving Robin a big smile. As always, when Vanessa felt insecure, she was even more charming then usual.

Robin clapped his hands, and stood next to her.

"Oh you shall do nicely as well! Fret not, Lady charisma! You, too, shall have abilities beyond the ken of mortal men."

He then grinned at her cheekily.

"Promise not to enslave too many of them, if you please? People tend to get suspicious!"

Vanessa smiled back at him, confused but enjoying his carefree appearance. "Thank you, kind sir. I only hope I discover these abilities soon, in order to better aid my sister in fighting the approaching darkness."

Robin stood up, cocked his head as though listening to something, then clapped his hands again.

"Your teacher arrives! I must be off. Much to do today, no time to play!"

With those cryptic words, he vanished right in front of them, as he had the previous time.

Cat looked at Vanessa, who still appeared confused but hopeful now. Finally, what they'd been waiting for. But who was the teacher Robin had promised? They could see no one and even the dandelions had calmed with the disappearance of the breeze. Suddenly, the clearing began to darken and a great wind whipped around the girls. Just as Cat began to get frightened, a huge eagle dropped out of the sky and landed in the clearing. As it touched the ground they watched it transform into a beautiful woman. The girls stood stunned, staring as she straightened up and shook out a feathered dress.

Her voice was harsh but still musical, much deeper then Glory's had been, and powerful.

"Good day, daughters of man. I see two with great power, one as yet sleeping." Both Vanessa and Cat dropped into a curtsey, feeling as though they were in the presence of a queen.

"Rise, daughters. I am here to act as a guide for the daughter of the wind."

Vanessa stood up then spoke in a calm and falsely bold voice.

"Thank you, Madame. My name is Vanessa McLean, and this is my sister, Catherine. We are deeply indebted to you for your aid."

Vanessa stood proudly, waiting for the woman to speak again.

"You may call me Aurora. I will show you the power of the air and you will learn your abilities. I will come to you at night, as the firebird does, and you will learn then. Now you must go. The hour grows late and you have much to do."

She handed Vanessa a feather from her dress.

"You will need this to link to me at night. Keep it safe, and keep it close."

Without further explanation, the woman then stretched her arms wide, lifting straight up while transforming, and disappeared back into the sky.

Vanessa and Cat stood blankly looking at each other until Cat cleared her throat. "Man! Each time I've been here things are totally weird. Let's go home. Time moves differently here and we've likely been away for hours already."

Vanessa nodded and they turned back to the tree, following the path back home.

LUCKILY, THEY'D GONE during the day this time, and weren't expected back yet. Vanessa looked happy for the first time in a long while and chatted excitedly once they were back to the human world.

"Did you see that? It was amazing! I can't wait to go to sleep tonight. Finally, I can be more useful in this fight. And Robin said I would be powerful. What do you think I can do?"

Vanessa looked at Cat eagerly, waiting for a reply.

Cat just shrugged.

"I haven't got a clue. I'm not sure what a wind power can do. I'm really not sure what any power can do, to be perfectly honest. So far I've spent most of my time muddling through my own abilities. But I'm very happy you've finally talked to someone. I hope you have dreams as amazing as mine."

Vanessa smiled and hugged herself as they talked, but they soon fell silent while thinking of their own respective abilities. By the time they got home, they were more than happy to see night fall. They said goodnight early, parting ways at their bedrooms in anticipation of the night ahead.

This time, they both dreamed. Cat continued to learn about what she could do with Glory, while Vanessa had a chance to meet with Aurora for her first lesson.

VANESSA HAD FALLEN asleep quickly, finding herself back in the clearing standing in front of the eagle again, who shook herself into the form of the woman she'd seen that afternoon.

"Good evening, Wind-walker," the woman said, inclining her head regally.

"Good evening, Madame," Vanessa replied, tingling with anticipation, eager to know everything all at once.

"Let us start with the basics. First, you must learn to see."

The woman stepped closer and touched Vanessa's forehead in the middle, where many cultures believe the location of the third eye to be, and Vanessa felt a rush of sensations. A feeling of flying and a multitude of images raced through her head, and she felt herself fade to black.

Vanessa blinked in the sunlight streaming across her face. When she was finally able to keep her eyes open, she found herself back in her room. The sounds of her mom getting ready downstairs intruded on her still foggy mind. As she lay there, everything from the night came back to her in pieces. She felt in tune with the air now and realized she could see the air currents in her room if she looked closely. As she looked around, she saw a bird outside her open window catch a gust of air and she blew softly toward it. As she did, the bird begin to move faster. Delighted, she got up and got dressed, eager to go outside and try out her new gift.

"PSSST CAT! ARE YOU awake?"

Cat was still lying in bed, sound asleep as Vanessa peered into her room. She went over and poked her.

"Mmmmm," Cat groaned. "What do you waaaaaant?"

She blinked her eyes blearily to see who was bothering her.

"I want to go play outside!" said Vanessa, as she jostled her sister.

Cat sat up and rubbed her eyes.

"What did you do? What happened?"

Suddenly she was awake and interested.

"I learned so much last night! I want to go to the park and see what I can do. It's still early, so hopefully no one's around yet."

Vanessa was positively bouncing with impatience.

Cat nodded.

"Okay, give me five minutes and I'll be right down."

They let their parents know where they were heading and took off into the early spring morning. Vanessa was so happy she felt as if she was floating, at least, until Cat gasped, prompting Vanessa to look at her.

"What?" she said, confused and looking around.

"Vanessa, you're floating!"

Cat pointed at her feet and Vanessa looked down. She was about two inches off the ground, abruptly dropping onto the sidewalk when she looked.

Vanessa gave a little squeal and danced.

"This is awesome!"

Cat smiled, happy to see Vanessa was finally getting to use her new powers. She'd been trying to figure out what they were for so long they'd both been starting to think Grandma had been wrong about her. They found an isolated part of the park that was shaded by a patch of trees, where Cat turned to her sister.

"Okay, now what?" she said, waiting to hear what needed to be done so early on a weekend.

"I want to see if I can use the wind. Aurora showed me how last night, but it may be different in real life."

"Go for it. No one's here and I'm super curious to see what you can do."

Cat waved her arm to emphasize her words.

Vanessa nodded, closed her eyes, and concentrated on the wind touching her face. She thought about making the breeze harder and about making herself lighter. She opened her eyes to see she was hovering again. She lifted her arms, and felt it catch under her. Flying! She was actually sort of flying, not quite, but sort of.

Cat was watching with her mouth open, but managed to collect herself.

"This is great! Um, maybe you should come down in case someone sees you. What else can you do?"

Vanessa slowly floated down to the ground then focused on the breeze again. This time she started stirring her arms in the air, which caused it to whip around in circles like a small tornado.

"Awesome!"

Cat clapped, and Vanessa dropped her arms again.

"According to Aurora, I also have the ability to charm people. I have powers similar to a sylph, once I learn how to use them."

Cat looked at her sister's aura again and saw a strong purple glow, more intense than before.

"This is great! Between your powers and mine, we may actually stand a chance against Declan."

Vanessa beamed with pride and stopped showing off. They continued walking, discussing the new skills they'd learned the night before.

The girls filled Evelyn in on the news during lunch at school on Monday. She was suitably impressed and jealous.

"Man, why couldn't I have something cooler than just knowing stuff sometimes. You guys suck."

Cat and Vanessa smirked at each other.

"Are you guys going to go to the rehearsal tonight?" Vanessa asked.

Vanessa, of course, was in the play, but Cat and Evelyn had been doing the props, so they weren't required to be there.

"Of course!" said Evelyn. "How will I be able to make sure everything is where it needs to be? Just because some homicidal sociopath may kill us all doesn't give this production an excuse to be sloppy!"

She said it as a joke, but Cat knew she really meant it.

Cat crossed her arms.

"Yeah, I'll be there. I want to scope out the set-up so I know where an attack could come from."

Although she was feeling more hopeful every day with how far they'd come with their own abilities, they still knew next to nothing about Declan. She felt a pit in her stomach threaten to swallow the joy of the moment and ruthlessly shoved it away.

# CHAPTER
# FOURTEEN THE
# REHEARSAL

REHEARSAL WEEK HUMMED with excitement. For most of the student body, classes were light that week. The teachers had given up on teaching and exams were starting soon, so most of the staff were only holding review classes. Cat and Evelyn weren't overly worried about marks for their Grade Ten finals, but Vanessa wanted to get on the honour roll. Although now that she knew about her extra abilities she was seriously reconsidering college, thinking she stood a decent chance of success in Hollywood. If she had half the charisma she was supposed to develop with practice, she could be the next big thing within a few years.

Cat couldn't believe it was almost the end of the year. She'd learned so much about herself and the world, none of it school related. She'd made a friend, always something she struggled with, and she was closer to her family, especially her sister. Overall not a bad year. Except that whole time spent in a coma, she thought wryly.

Drama practice was at six that night. It was the first run through, which meant no costumes, but everything else needed to be done as it would be for opening night. People had to know their cues and all of the actors needed to be there, including understudies. This made for a crowded auditorium, with people sitting in the seats and almost as many backstage. Cat had been acting as Evelyn's right hand, basically moving stuff when she was told to, so they were both backstage as Vanessa chatted with the other actors.

Evelyn stopped directing people mid-order, turning to look at Cat with a strange expression.

"Cat, Declan isn't here yet. Something's wrong."

Cat felt queasy when she looked at her friend. She knew Evelyn was more accurate with her 'feelings' than she was and the fact that he hadn't shown was worrisome.

"Maybe he's running late?" she offered, lamely, not surprised when Evelyn gave her a look of disbelief.

"Or maybe he's sucking the life out of someone."

Evelyn put her hands on her hips, waiting for Cat to do something. Cat sighed, getting up from fixing the base of a tree.

"Okay, fine. I'll see if I can scope out the school and find him."

Evelyn looked slightly mollified. Cat whispered a quick update to Vanessa before slipping out of the crowded stage area into the hallway.

She stood in the dimly lit hall silently, waiting to hear anything unusual. A locker shut nearby and Cat crammed herself behind a plant to wait. As she'd expected, Declan sauntered by looking relaxed and carefree. She waited until he'd passed her hiding place and entered the auditorium, before she snuck down the hallway in the direction he'd come from, peaking over her shoulder to make sure he hadn't returned.

In between the lockers, beside the English classroom, a figure lay slumped on the floor. The way they were crumpled in a corner made it difficult to make out who the person was at first. As she approached, Cat was appalled to see Ms. Fisk. She appeared to be unconscious, and her colour was an unhealthy grey. Cat snapped into aura-vision almost without thinking. What she could see of the teacher's aura was dark and had the appearance of death, being almost completely gone.

Cat felt the familiar heat rise in her chest and placed her hands over her teacher's heart. She concentrated all of her energy into her hands and thrust it into the woman on the floor, bringing life back into her with the fire in her soul. As she worked, Ms. Fisk's colour improved and her breathing evened out. The black was erased by the light Cat poured into her, until finally her eyes opened.

Ms. Fisk looked at her with confusion.

"What? Where am I? Cat? What are you doing here?"

She looked around as though she was lost.

"Where did Declan go? Oh, I'm so embarrassed! I must have fainted or something..."

Her voice trailed off. As she looked at Cat, her eyes flooded with memory and she shook her head.

"No, that's not what happened," she said, slowly starting to piece the events together. "I was talking to Declan then his eyes became dark and cold, and I felt like I'd fallen into a well. I knew I wouldn't ever be able to get out. I didn't even know if I was still breathing."

Ms. Fisk stood up shakily, and Cat helped to steady her. She looked up at Cat with a steely, questioning gaze.

"You saved my life, didn't you? What are you?" she said, laughing humourlessly, then added, "Hell, what is *he*? What in the name of God is going on here?"

Cat shrugged, not sure what or how much to say.

"It's kind of difficult to explain, but he's very dangerous. You should probably avoid being too close to him again."

Ms. Fisk looked her over closely for a few minutes before shaking her head tiredly in acceptance.

"I think I'm going to go home and have a nice warm bath. If I feel up to it, I may want to ask you some questions tomorrow."

She grimaced then rubbed her eyes as if to wipe away her memories.

"On second thought, I may not want to know. I might decide to pretend this never happened."

Cat released her hand that she'd used to steady the teacher and Ms. Fisk gave her a spontaneous hug.

"Thanks, Cat. I owe you."

She gave her another tight squeeze then walked out without a backward glance.

Cat watched until she'd left the building, still shaky from what had almost happened. This was way beyond anything Declan had done in public in a place where he was known and she was certain it had been the first attack in the upcoming war. She returned to drama practice, making a beeline for Evelyn.

"How's everything?"

Evelyn looked at her curiously, waiting for report, since she'd sent her to look in the first place.

Cat looked around, lowering her voice before replying.

"Declan just took out Ms. Fisk!"

Evelyn dropped the prop she'd been holding, covering her mouth in shock. "What? No way! Is she...okay?"she asked, her eyes wide with worry.

Cat nodded.

"Yeah, I got to her in time but it was close, Evelyn. She almost died. I don't think my abilities extend that far. As it was, it totally wore me out. It's the most tired I've been after a healing in a long time."

Evelyn shook her head in dismay.

"I can't believe he did that here, in the school, so close to the big event. That's either really, really ballsy, or just plain stupid. Or maybe he doesn't care anymore, because he doesn't think anyone will be able stop him."

Cat agreed.

"That's what I'm scared of. It's coming up so fast. I hope we're ready for it."

Evelyn's normally vibrant face became clouded with concern.

"I'm worried what he'll do if he finds out about us before the 18th."

Cat sighed, shoulders slumped, hands going into her pockets as she looked at her friend.

"Me too, Evelyn. Me too."

AFTER THE RUN-THROUGH, Vanessa drove the girls home. Cat and Evelyn filled her in on the hidden events of the night and she turned a shade paler when she heard the circumstances.

"God, I'm glad you went to check. This is too much. What are we going to do?"

Cat looked at her with her jaw set.

"We're going to do what we need to do. We'll go to the opening night of the play and we'll stop Declan. No matter what it takes, we *will* succeed, somehow."

With only two days left, and a rehearsal every night, including the final dress rehearsal, the girls were busy and stretched for time. Vanessa and Cat worked during the night in their dreams, honing their new abilities with their twilight tutors.

Declan seemed to have stepped up his attacks to a new level, perhaps in preparation for the coming big day. Evelyn continued to bring increasingly frightening news from her mother. The hospital was overrun with admissions for new strokes and altered level of consciousness, as well as from a rash of car accidents and unexplained sudden deaths. Most hadn't made it into news reports or people would have started to notice that something was off and begun to panic. Many of the events had been chalked up to alcohol or drugs, and a rumour had started to go around of a dealer selling bad product tainted with fentanyl.

Cat and Vanessa had received information from their guides about what to watch for and had been told that Declan planned to do whatever it was in the middle of the play. The guides had warned the girls he would start by clouding the minds of everyone present, and that they'd need to be on guard to ensure he didn't trap them as well. They shared the information with Evelyn, hoping if they were all aware and ready they wouldn't succumb, otherwise their plan would fail before it began.

The night of the dress rehearsal came, and the girls were all nervous. The last night before whatever Declan had planned came to fruition. Vanessa, of course, had to be on stage as one of the main characters, so she'd be unable to watch or leave if the situation escalated. Evelyn and Cat were free to come and go as part of the backstage crew and Cat had already scoped the hallways to hopefully avoid a repeat event like the one concerning Ms. Fisk. In the middle of their set up for the play, Evelyn had another feeling and left to call her mom. When she came back, her face was drawn and ashen.

"What's wrong?"

Cat didn't like the look on her friend's face and when she spoke every drop of colour drained from Evelyn's face.

"There's been another car accident, but this time it was your parents."

Evelyn spoke quietly, trying not to panic her friend, holding her hands out in a calming gesture.

Cat dropped her bag on the floor, her hands suddenly powerless.

"What? No. Are they okay?"

Evelyn shook her head.

"They're alive, but Mom says they're acting 'off', the way people are after Declan's drained them. She told me to tell you to get over there, ASAP. And take Vanessa. You both need to go."

Cat nodded and walked on numb legs over to the drama teacher. He patted her shoulder awkwardly then pulled Vanessa aside while giving her understudy the nod to take over. As Cat watched the interaction, she noticed Declan standing off to the side, smiling slightly at the look on Vanessa's face as the teacher told her the news. Declan shifted his gaze to Cat, giving her a brief but intense look full of loathing before he blinked and appeared completely innocent again.

Vanessa came running over, breaking the weird eye contact with Declan.

"What do you know?" she asked, breathlessly.

She looked at Cat pleadingly, wringing her hands as she waited for a reply.

Cat shrugged.

"Not much. Evelyn felt something was wrong and called her mom who's working tonight. She said they came into the ER from a car accident and Marie-Jean wants us there right now, because they aren't acting normally."

Vanessa nodded impatiently.

"Well, what are we doing here then? Let's go."

She looked around.

"Where's Evelyn?"

Cat scanned the room, unable to see her through the mass of people and props backstage.

"I'm not sure. I don't see her anymore."

Vanessa took a look herself before huffing and shaking her head.

"Let's go, I can't wait. I need to see them."

Cat almost agreed, given that Evelyn had told them to leave right away, but hesitated. The look Declan had given her had made her blood run even colder than it usually did when she saw him. It was a look of someone who absolutely hated her and wished her dead.

"No, we can't leave without her. He must know we're stopping him from getting his usual victim count."

Vanessa groaned in frustration, and Cat quickly ran down the mental list.

"Think about it. What with you, Ms. Fisk, and now our parents? The only thing you all have in common is me. He's seen both you and Ms. Fisk walking around, healed from whatever he did to you. Even if he can't feel it, you guys aren't acting the way people usually do after he's gotten to them."

"Ugh. You're right, I know you are. Of course he'd want you out of the way, or better yet, dead, if he knew you were messing up his stuff. So, I guess we shouldn't let Evelyn out of our sight either."

Vanessa still looked wired, but her shoulders had relaxed slightly and Cat knew she agreed with her.

"No," Cat said, shaking her head. "We can't get separated now. We have to assume Declan knows we're onto him, or at least he knows I'm doing something, and I don't want him getting to Evelyn this close to the tribute."

Vanessa looked determined and nodded.

"Okay, so let's find her fast."

Cat led the way from backstage and they luckily spotted Evelyn just outside the back door of the auditorium, bag packed and ready.

"Here I am. Lets go, I've got my mom's car out back. I know a short-cut to the hospital."

The three girls loaded into the small red Ford Tempo, with Evelyn in the driver's seat. It seemed to take forever to get to the hospital, although when Cat looked at her watch, only a few minutes had passed.

Evelyn dropped them off at the emergency entrance doors.

"Go ahead. I'll park and be right in."

Cat hesitated.

"Go," Evelyn said, sharply. "I'll be fine and you can come looking if I'm not there in five minutes."

Evelyn could see the doubt in her face and reiterated.

"I promise I'll be fine. He's still at school, remember?"

Cat reluctantly nodded, accepting the odds before following Vanessa, who'd already hopped out and raced inside the building through the sliding doors.

IT WAS A COMPLETE MADHOUSE inside the ER this time. Every bed was full and the medical staff were running in all directions. Cat and Vanessa looked around for someone to speak to, but everyone they saw was urgently attending to call bells or patients. As they waited at the desk, Cat noticed one of the trauma bay curtains was slightly open. She caught a glimpse of her dad's pale face behind it and pinched Vanessa's arm. She turned to scowl at Cat, who pointed at the curtained area. Vanessa gasped and they rushed over, pulling the curtain the rest of the way back. Their parents lay on stretchers side by side, covered in blood.

Cat had the image of her injured parents burned into her mind and knew she wouldn't forget it for a long time. Yet as the shock faded, she was able to catalogue what she saw more dispassionately. They were breathing and awake and she didn't see any obvious injuries. What she did see was a complete lack of reaction to their daughters' presence in the room, with only vacant stares at the ceiling as though they were trapped in their own heads.

Cat felt the power rise up in her chest and lifted her arms. Vanessa quickly pulled the curtain back around to hide them from public viewing. As Cat began to channel her power through her hands, a nurse peeked around the curtain. Vanessa nodded in relief upon seeing Marie-Jean, and waved her in. Evelyn's mom stood at the doorway, looking on with frustrated anger while acting as a physical barrier to anyone entering the sick bay. Cat felt more secure with her protection and placing her hands on both of her parents heads, let her firebird soar.

The air crackled around her as Vanessa and Marie-Jean watched with awe. Cat's long red hair had broken free of its perpetual ponytail and was floating around her within the static. Her entire body was glowing and light poured from her hands into her parents' bodies. As Vanessa and Marie-Jean looked on, comprehension returned to the eyes of the figures on the stretchers, who both blinked.

Cat dropped her arms and her hair cascaded back limply over her shoulders as she staggered. She caught hold of the railings of both beds, panting weakly until Vanessa waved her arm and a chair moved beneath Cat. She sat down while Marie-Jean nodded at them approvingly.

"I see you've both come a long way. About time, I must say. Evelyn says the big day is tomorrow."

Vanessa went over to the other side of her dad's stretcher.

"Dad? Are you okay?"

He gave Vanessa a weak smile.

"I feel fine, now, but it was absolutely awful."

He still looked pale.

"What happened?" Vanessa and Cat asked in unison, as Evelyn slipped in and gave her mother a hug.

Cat was relieved to see she was safe, but needed to hear what had happened and turned back to her dad.

He looked confused as he tried to explain what had happened, as most people did after running into Declan.

"Your mother and I were out getting supper. We thought since you two were out for the evening we'd have a nice little date, just the two of us. As we were leaving to go home, we were stopped by a young man. He asked if we were your parents and when we said yes, everything went black. I felt like I'd fallen into a dark hole. I don't remember exactly what happened, but I think he touched us. The next thing I know, we were hitting a tree with the car. I don't even remember getting behind the wheel. And now here you two are."

He looked at his girls proudly with eyes full of love.

"You both are so incredible. Your Grandma would be so proud of how far you've come."

"I agree, dear."

Cat and Vanessa turned to look at their mom with trepidation. While they'd mostly kept their dad in the loop about what they were doing with their new powers, they hadn't said anything to their mom. It had been somewhat deliberate, but also merely part of not really knowing what to say or how she'd take it. She smiled at them, chiding them gently when she saw their surprise.

"Oh guys, you think I didn't know what was going on? Please! I've been married to your dad for 20 years and I knew your grandmother. I may not have a great deal of otherworldly talent myself, but I'm an artist. We tend to see things that others don't, remember?"

"Good point," Vanessa said, smiling ruefully before giving her a hug. "Do you remember anything else? With your perceptive artist's eye?"

Her mom thought for a minute then answered slowly, appearing to find the words as she spoke.

"Pretty much what your dad said, although I'm pretty sure I saw the young man looking quite satisfied and I think I heard him say something like 'there, that should keep her busy for awhile' as he left us."

She looked over to Cat.

"I'm guessing based on that remarkable bit of power you just displayed, he was talking about you? Have you been messing up his work lately? He seemed sort of disgruntled."

Cat shrugged.

"I've been healing as many of his victims as I can and as I've been healing I've been getting more powerful. It's getting easier, so I guess I'm also speeding up. I think he's figured it out and probably hoped this diversion would keep us out of his way until after the play tomorrow. We think he plans to steal the souls of everyone who goes tomorrow night."

Her dad nodded.

"That makes sense. He probably knows you can heal, but not how powerful you are. Taking out your mother and I, either temporarily or permanently had we actually died in that crash, would have distracted you. Possibly long enough for him to succeed."

Marie-Jean agreed, with a solemn shake of her head.

"Well, he's obviously not ready for our girls then, if he thinks this will slow them down."

Evelyn still looked troubled.

"What is it?" Vanessa asked, her head tilted in an attempt to read her.

Evelyn shook her head before slowly exhaling and looking at them. "I think it's more than that. I think he needs the souls tomorrow, but what if he also needs to prepare for the tribute and wants us out of the way? It'd make sense if he has to start the ritual tonight. It's the new moon and almost completely dark outside. Maybe it ties into his birthday somehow and it's part of the transfer of power."

She turned to look at Cat, still working through her thoughts as she spoke.

"Cat, didn't you say you read about the moon being hit by a meteor or something on the day he was born? Maybe that's why he was picked for this. Maybe the dark figure that gave Declan his powers caused that crater to happen on the moon. Is that even possible?"

Cat raised her shoulders in the universal gesture signifying uncertainty.

"I've got no idea. It could be. It would definitely tie everything together. Maybe we should swing by his house on the way home tonight and see if we can snoop around and find out anything else."

Everyone in the room looked uncomfortable, but her mom broke the silence.

"I think if you feel there's a chance to find out what to do and how to stop what's going to happen tomorrow night, you should go. But you should stay together and be careful. It's crucial you aren't discovered and I don't think I need to warn you to stay out of sight."

Their dad and Marie-Jean nodded.

"Evelyn," Marie-Jean serenely added, as though giving a benediction, "you'll be the early warning. If you have any bad feelings, I want you to leave. Vanessa, you can be the weapon, and Cat you're the shield."

Marie-Jean spelled out their roles simply. Cat had never thought of it in those terms before, but when she heard it put that way, she felt more confident about their chance of success. Together, they would be an unstoppable team.

Marie-Jean promised to keep their parents safe in hospital until the morning and after hugging them and saying goodbye, the girls set out towards Declan's house. They remembered it only too well from the night of the party. They cautiously parked on the street across and a few houses down, so they weren't visible from the front of his home. They sat in the dark for a few moments, each struck by the sheer inertia of not wanting to embark upon what they were about to do.

After a long silence, Cat spoke.

"So, are we going to do this?"

Evelyn and Vanessa groaned and grudgingly unbuckled their seatbelts.

"I don't want to go back to that house," Vanessa said, shuddering with the memory of the last time she'd been there.

Evelyn nodded sympathetically.

"I totally get that. Why don't we go down the back lane and see if we can look into the yard from there? That way, if anyone sees us we can pretend we're just out walking."

Cat and Vanessa concurred and they all got out of the car. They ducked around to the back alley at the corner of the street, walking as quietly as they could. They took care not to skip any stones with their feet or disturb any of the dried leaves on the ground. Vanessa used the breeze to bend one of the branches on a huge oak tree behind the fence so that she could float up onto it, then just as gently bent it back up. If Cat hadn't known better, she would have thought Vanessa was riding an escalator.

Cat and Evelyn watched her from the road as she crouched down low in the tree, completely concealed by leaves. She sat there for a minute before floating back over the fence, this time without the aid of the branch.

"There are some large bushes next to the fence on the other side. It looks like a good place to stay hidden. I don't see anything yet, but maybe we can wait there?"

Evelyn bowed her head slightly.

"I think Declan needs to be outside tonight, and I think it'll be happening soon. Let's wait there."

Settled on the plan, they carefully crept into their new hiding place and waited.

IT FELT LIKE AN INTERMINABLY long time, but by the light on her watch Cat saw it was only 9:30. Just when she thought they weren't going to see anything after all, Evelyn grabbed her arm and put her finger to her lips. Cat settled back down, trying to hide as best as she could beneath the leaves. She hadn't noticed him at first, as she'd become used to using her aura vision to see people approaching when her eyes couldn't see in the dark. Since Declan had no aura, he was practically invisible to her. But as she watched the light spill out from the doorway, he walked calmly down the back stairs. For the first time, she noticed a small stone circle in the middle of the yard, with a fireplace in it's centre.

Declan was so dark and quiet he almost blended into the night, but as he walked to the fireplace it suddenly blazed into life. He started to talk, but Cat couldn't make out what he was saying. Then from out of the fire the tall, hooded figure she remembered from her dream stepped into reality. Cat felt her blood turn to ice in her veins, as her hearing became hyper-acute.

The figure spoke in a deep, cold, and menacing voice.

"Are you ready for the tribute, vassal?" he said condescendingly, as though speaking to a servant he cared nothing for. Which was likely the case, Cat thought, unable to tear her eyes away.

Declan bowed deeply at the figure, responding obsequiously.

"Yes, sir. It shall be as planned. During the play, I will give my speech as Robin Goodfellow and shroud the audience with fog. They'll be meek as sheep then and you shall be well happy with the take I will be able to get."

The dark figure seemed to menace larger.

"Remember, you must claim more souls then the last tribute. You have been running sadly behind as of late with the souls you should have already taken and will need to account for that as well."

Declan practically growled in response.

"Stupid female. There's a girl. I don't know what or how she is doing it, but she's thwarting my powers somehow. I believe I've taken care of her for the tribute, at least. I've claimed her parents with your dark mark and they may even be dead now. It's doubtful she'll be a problem tomorrow and if she is, I'll simply take care of her then."

The figure turned, dramatically swirling his cloak.

"I hope for your sake that you are right or this will be your final tribute. And you will not like where you are going if you fail." With those ominous words, the figure vanished back into the fire. Declan waited for a moment before putting out the fire, looking angry as he did so, before disappearing back into the house.

The girls waited for another 20 minutes before slowly and carefully leaving the back yard. No one spoke until they were in the car and even after that it was several minutes until any of them could find words to discuss what they'd seen.

When they finally did, it was Vanessa who spoke first.

"So, um, woah, hey guys? Did you catch the surprise visitor? Pretty scary, hey?" Cat and Evelyn nodded without answering. They all sat for a little longer, not moving.

"I'm totally not going to be able to sleep tonight. My mom's on a night shift. Can I stay with you guys? I don't want to be alone."

Evelyn looked scared for the first time since they'd known her. Cat smiled, trying to comfort her friend when she had the same fears.

"Of course. We need to stick together until this is over. We don't want to give him any extra opportunities to hurt us, and together we're stronger."

# CHAPTER FIFTEEN
# THE PLAY

EVELYN HAD BEEN RIGHT. Even with them staying together, they didn't get a great sleep that night. Both Vanessa and Cat's teachers were no-shows, so they were left to deal with their own troubled dreams instead. It was really and truly up to them either way, sink or swim. When the morning came, the girls grudgingly and tiredly got up to face it. With no parents to monitor them, they ate very little. The idea of food was more than Cat could handle, with her stomach full of butterflies already.

The school day was incredibly painful for all of them. It took an eternity for classes to pass, but luckily it was only a half day. They were let out right after lunch, which meant they didn't have to pretend to pay attention the entire day, only during the morning. Set up for the play started early, with Cat and Evelyn helping with auditorium prop placement, and Vanessa running through lines with the other actors.

Cat kept a close watch on her, but with everyone present except the actual audience, she wasn't too concerned yet. It would be during the height of the play, with maximum occupancy, when she expected everything to go down. After all, according to Declan himself, he would do it during one of Puck's speeches. She also knew the warning signal would be a cloud or fog of some kind, if they'd correctly understood Declan's irritated words of the night before.

Cat found herself growing increasingly tense as the debut drew near. She was a little disappointed that she wouldn't get a chance to actually watch and enjoy the play, considering how much work everyone had put into the preparations. It would almost certainly be the first and last night of the production, regardless of whether they were successful or not. After all, one of the stars, if not more, would be out of action when it was all over. And that was assuming things went well. If Declan succeeded, no one would be around to stage or watch the play in the future. Cat had made her parents promise to stay far away once they got out of the hospital, so at least she and Vanessa didn't have to worry about them as well. It was all so big, and absolutely crazy.

Cat leaned over to Evelyn and whispered.

"How the heck did we get here? And why us?"

Evelyn patted her shoulder, indicating a shared perplexity.

"I don't know. I guess at the end of the day, someone has to do it. As they say in show biz, the show must go on."

Evelyn flashed her a tight smile before looking around and waving her hand at the general backstage area.

"We still have a lot of work to do. The whole good versus evil, balance in the universe stuff has to wait until we get these people going."

Cat rubbed her face wearily.

"Yeah, I know. Blah, blah, blah. It's like the crap they tell you when you're a kid and you have to get needles."

She shook her head and helped Evelyn move another tree into place. The conversation died as they focused on the work, but Cat kept a nervous eye at the clock, feeling the countdown continue.

People started to meander into the auditorium at 6:30. Everything was so banal, as students accepted tickets and showed people to their seats and everyone milled around chatting with their neighbours instead of sitting. The atmosphere was pleasant and full of a low grade excitement for the play ahead. It made things even more surreal for the girls and staying composed was difficult.

Vanessa was putting on her best actress face, and her charisma was off the charts. Cat hardly thought it was fair, but one of the new abilities her sister now had, in addition to her already mad people skills, was the ability to be amazingly charismatic and act as a muse to others.

In Cat's estimation, it basically meant that if Vanessa decided to marry rich, she could. Or if she wanted to be an actress, a model, or anything else that involved the opinion or admiration of others, she would be able to.

Evelyn was busy bossing everyone around, which was something that she excelled at, but it also made her more comfortable. She appeared more alert than usual but the average observer would probably simply chalk it up to the stress of the event. After what seemed to be only a few moments, the lights flashed the ten minute warning and people began to settle into their chairs. Cat's stomach flipped over when the lights turned off. Vanessa was separated from the other two girls, but they managed to keep in touch backstage through the occasional visual and tried to stay as physically near by as possible without being in the way. Declan was his normal affable, friendly self with everyone back stage, and the girls did their best not to act unusual around him, and he acted like they weren't even there.

Then the play started. A hush fell over the audience. Cat felt like puking with the tension and had to calm herself. She tried to keep some warmth in her body so she'd be ready to heal but felt ice cold with nerves. It was going to take all the strength she had. She watched as the interwoven plot lines unfolded, with the two sets of lovers, the wedding play, and the overall hijinks that ensued. She felt herself on the tips of her toes as Declan gave the speech about it all being a dream.

At that moment, a faint mist crept up and drifted over the audience. As she watched, she saw people in the light emanating from stage. Their eyes seemed to glaze over and their faces became slack, almost dreamy. She couldn't hear the words Declan was speaking at that point, so moved in order to hear them more clearly. She caught Evelyn's eye, nodding her head. She needed a better view of the audience so she could heal, if needed, and so she could monitor what Declan was doing.

As Cat moved, Vanessa saw her and edged to stage left. She appeared to be concentrating, her hands slightly raised, and Cat felt a breeze brush her hair. Declan didn't notice until a few minutes passed, but when he did he looked around, perplexed by the fog dissipating from the audience. Cat was now out of sight, knowing it wasn't yet her moment to act. She was hoping Vanessa could make the evil miasma disappear with her powers alone and it looked good until Declan straightened up. He appeared determined and angry and Cat knew it wasn't over. She could now hear what he was saying and listening to his words she realized he was completely off script, reciting what sounded like a ritualized offering instead.

"Hear me, Oh Dark One, tonight on the anniversary of your blessing, I offer to you the Tribute of Souls, in accordance with our agreement. May you receive of these souls and be satisfied."

The audience had remained placid and dreamy, but Cat watched in horror as their auras moved towards Declan. People began to slump over in their seats and Cat stepped forward. She couldn't wait any longer. It was time to act. She saw Vanessa and Evelyn looking frightened backstage but Cat shoved the image away. She let her chest fill with the warmth of a healing, but this time instead of thinking about the people in the audience, she aimed it squarely at Declan.

She thought of the person he'd once been, before he'd been visited by darkness, and the night she'd seen him as a young, sick human. As she filled with light, she felt herself lift and realized Vanessa was helping with her wind power, bringing her level with Declan. He'd noticed her now, and was livid at the interference.

"You!" he snarled, his face twisting into an evil looking scowl. "What are you? What have you been doing to me?"

For the first time Cat could remember, he sounded like a petulant 18 year old. "Why won't you leave me alone?"

It was this combination of frustration and whining that made Cat relax. He was just a boy, although a very old one to be sure, and was accustomed to getting his own way, even if it wasn't good for him.

"You know who I am, Declan. I'm simply undoing what you've been doing to people for centuries. You've taken what isn't yours for so long you've forgotten you don't deserve it. Tonight, I'll help you remember that."

And with those words, Cat turned all her focus onto Declan and into healing his soul. As she worked, she felt the now familiar tingle begin in her chest, moving outwards through her hands and exploding out of her.

As Vanessa and Evelyn watched from the sidelines, light poured out of Cat's fingertips and her hair swirled like fire around her head. Vanessa moved Cat closer to Declan with the wind so she could touch him. Cat was hardly even aware at this point of anything other than her target, but reached out and touched his chest over his heart. The light poured out of her into him and everything exploded around them. Cat and Declan split apart, falling backward on the stage.

Vanessa and Evelyn felt the pressure change, as though their ears had just equalized. After a few seconds, Declan and Cat began to recover on the floor. Cat inhaled deeply several times, feeling as if she was going to hurl, but Declan appeared to be bewildered.

He stood up and saw the girls on stage with him, and stared at them in confusion. "What are you doing here? What just happened?"

Vanessa stepped closer, reading the green tint on Cat's face and her rapid breathing as clues that she wasn't in any condition to answer yet.

"Healing you, I hope," said Vanessa.

Cat smiled weakly at her sister in gratitude then looked closely at Declan. A faint glow of an aura now surrounded him, and while it wasn't much, it was there, glowing in a strong silver tone.

Declan looked down at himself in wonder.

"How did..."

But as they watched, his face crumpled with sadness mixed with fear.

"What have I done? All these years..." his sentence trailed off, and he looked at the audience for the first time. Luckily, they were still in the dream state into which he'd put them, unaware of the extremely odd goings on that weren't remotely related to the event they'd come to see.

Cat finally felt able to stand and feeling a familiar breeze under her arms, she knew that Vanessa was adding her support from beside her. She smiled at her gratefully. She looked at Declan's new aura, and realized that somehow, she'd given him back his soul. When she examined the audience, she could see that although they still appeared to be drugged, their souls had resettled, each person normal again except for their dreamy expressions.

Declan looked at Cat.

"I don't know how or what you've done, but after what I've done for the last thousand years... Well, it appears my time is up now and I must face my punishment".

Cat looked at him, frowning.

"Punishment?"

Declan smiled sadly.

"I once cheated the laws of man and nature, but now I must pay the price. The agreement was that I must steal souls at the cost of my own, and now it will be forfeit. I hadn't missed it before, as it wasn't on me to miss, but now that you've restored it somehow, I realize what I've done. And what's in store for me now that I have no souls to offer the dark master tonight. He shall take mine forever, as well as my life."

Declan looked at her, this time with beautiful bright blue eyes which were full of regret.

"I'm very sorry for what I've done and while it won't be for long, thank you for giving me a chance to feel again. I didn't know what I was missing until now."

Declan looked out into the audience with resignation and Cat followed his gaze. Walking down the centre aisle was the same shadow dark figure she'd seen in her dream and in Declan's back yard. Fear crep over her skin in goosebumps.

The man stopped in the aisle in front of the stage and coldly bega to speak.

"So, you have failed me then."

Declan stepped forward, looking scared but resolved.

"Yes, I have. And I'm sorry for not realizing how wrong it was be fore now."

The man laughed cruelly.

"Wrong. Right! Such human concepts are unimportant and irrel evant. There is no such thing as wrong or right, only power. And no\ you have none, and belong to me."

As the girls watched, the man made a grabbing motion at the ai and Declan flew towards him. Just as quickly as he'd waved his hanc Declan was gone. Cat stared at the dark hooded man, unable to mov or say anything. She felt his gaze turn to her and under his cloak sh. could feel what she thought were eyes, burning into her skin.

He spoke again, this time directly to her.

"You have done this then, have you?"

This time, his voice sounded like an icy caress, which she foun\ even more frightening than his earlier angry cold tone. She nodded, un able to find her tongue.

"He would have been wise to find out about you before now. Bu no matter. I have more where that came from and you are not a bothe to me right now."

He waved his hand dismissively and she flinched, expecting hersel to disappear. He watched her for another second or two.

"You have amused me tonight. But be careful you do not amuse m again, as I may not be so lenient next time."

This time, when he moved his arm his cloak billowed up around him, before he vanished.

Vanessa ran over to Cat and jump-hugged her.

"Are you ok?"

Cat nodded.

"Yeah, I'm fine."

She looked over at the audience members that were starting to move and could hear them murmuring about the scene on stage that they were witnessing.

"We need to get off stage now," Cat hissed.

Vanessa looked at the crowd and nodded.

"C'mon, let's get over here."

They managed to get backstage at the same time as the audience started to regain awareness and questions began in earnest. Vanessa left Cat and found the actors, who'd also been dazed, and somehow managed to convince everyone it was time for bows and curtain calls. The ruse went well considering, the only rough moment being when someone asked why Declan wasn't there. Evelyn used her considerable leadership skills to convince everyone that he was having diarrhea somewhere else, and the question was dropped. No one ever wanted details on diarrhea.

After everything was over, the play ended up being a big hit. Although no one wanted to admit that they couldn't remember what had happened at the end, people managed to convince themselves otherwise. Cat heard several differing opinions and found it amusing to listen to them. Most people knew the play so well that people believed they'd seen it based on their pre-existing knowledge. The next day she even saw that the reviewer from the local paper had given the play two thumbs up. Cat found it absolutely mind-blowing no one had any inkling about all the stuff that had happened right in front of their noses.

Of course, there were questions, and lots of them. No one seemed able to figure out where Declan had gone. It was as though they all vaguely remembered he'd said something, but couldn't quite remember what. Some people said he'd dropped out of school to join the military, others said that he was meeting up with his parents over in Europe somewhere. No one was bothered by his absence, which was interesting, as he'd been the most popular person in the high school the day before.

*But I guess when you're always sucking the energy out of people they don't miss you when you're gone.*

Their parents had wanted full details of course, and Cat and Vanessa had been more than happy to oblige them. They were impressed with themselves and wanted to tell someone what had gone down without sounding totally crazy. When they relayed the details of the evening, they could tell that their parents were simultaneously proud and horrified, which stroked the girls egos in a most satisfactory fashion.

Evelyn had been disappointed that she hadn't seen more 'active duty', as she described it, but Cat and Vanessa were quick to point out the many times leading up to the play that her second sense had kept them out of trouble or helped save someone, including Vanessa and Ms. Fisk.

Vanessa had surpassed what she'd believed herself capable of and everyone was proud of her. Considering that she'd only had a few weeks to figure out what to do with her powers, she'd blown Cat away, literally. Cat had also surpassed what she'd thought she could do, but only by degrees. In the end, it had been her choice to fight evil with compassion that had saved the day. Declan rediscovering a soul had changed his idea of right and wrong, but unfortunately that had cost him his life in the end, as he had bargained with it all those years ago.

The appearance by the hooded man had left the girls with huge questions, questions they didn't know what to do with. Why had he left them alone? He hadn't seemed upset, rather more amused by the fact that Cat had foiled his tribute, which scared her more than if he'd done something to them. It was as if he didn't think she was important enough to bother with. He also hadn't even registered Vanessa or Evelyn as present. They simply didn't matter to him. He'd made Declan vanish with no effort, as easily as if he was brushing hair off his face. And then he had stared at Cat and in that look she'd felt more coldness than she thought possible, along with fear that had crept right into her bones and stayed there. Then he'd vanished with a warning not to bother him again, or else. Or else what? The girls had talked it over constantly since the night of the play, but had been unable to draw any conclusions.

IN THE END, LIFE WENT on. The play's one-week run had finished to massive critical and popular acclaim, with the understudy for Puck bringing a boyish charm to the role that had been absent when Declan was in the role. They weren't sure who the boy was, but he reminded both Cat and Vanessa very much of the real Robin Goodfellow. Exams were written and passed, with both Evelyn and Cat moving on to Grade Eleven. They planned on picking the same class schedule for the following year so that they could stick together. For the first time she could remember, Cat had a friend she trusted like family and could rely on through anything. After all the bouncing around her family had done, this town felt like home. Her dad had promised she could finish high school there, no matter what happened with his job.

Vanessa was torn. She'd planned to move back to the city after school, but now she didn't want to leave Cat and Evelyn. They were in a new world together and were all excited to see what was out there. Seeing was believing for them and after meeting the likes of the dark hooded man, and seeing what a human with no soul was capable of, they wanted to figure out how to take the fight to the next level.

As they sat together on the back porch at Evelyn's place after the last day of school faded into memory, they sipped on iced tea and watched the sunset. Each had changed so much during the school year that they couldn't wrap their minds around it. Yet in the end, they had each other and they had their parents. And it was only the beginning.

Evelyn woke up, gasping for air. She looked around wildly, realizing she was home and still in her bed. The clock said 3:11. Her room was dark and still. She was alone in her room, but her mind remained full of the images that she'd seen. Fire, people crying, and a dark man, laughing coldly. She heard herself screaming and the man laughed louder.

*Oh God, no. I have to tell Cat and Vanessa.*

*He's coming.*

# Don't miss out!

Click the button below and you can sign up to receive emails whenever H. M. Gooden publishes a new book. There's no charge and no obligation.

https://books2read.com/r/B-A-POWE-JNDP

BOOKS 2 READ

Connecting independent readers to independent writers.

# About the Author

H. M. Gooden has always loved the world of books, but over the last few years a new story has begged to be told, and as a result, this book was born. In between dealing with children and work, the majority of her writing happens between four and six am and involves multiple cups of coffee for inspiration.

Read more at https://www.facebook.com/HMGoodenauthor/.

50356011R00117

Made in the USA
Middletown, DE
29 October 2017